The Boy's Own Guide to Fishing, Tackle-making and Fishbreeding

John Harrington Keene

BIBLIOBAZAAR

THE BOY'S OWN GUIDE

TO

FISHING

TACKLE-MAKING AND FISH-BREEDING

BEING A PLAIN, PRECISE AND PRACTICAL EXPLANATION
OF ALL THAT IS NECESSARY TO BE KNOWN
BY THE YOUNG ANGLER

BY

JOHN HARRINGTON KEENE

AUTHOR OF " THE PRACTICAL FISHERMAN " " FLY-FISHING AND FLY-MAKING "
" FISHING-TACKLE ITS MATERIALS AND MANUFACTURE " ETC.

*Illustrated by 82 diagrams drawn under the direct supervision
of the author by Lewis E. Shanks*

LEE AND SHEPARD PUBLISHERS
10 MILK STREET
BOSTON

ELECTROTYPING BY C. J. PETERS & SON, BOSTON, U.S.A.

PRESS OF S. J. PARKHILL & CO.

PREFACE

FISHING is a sport especially suited to boys. It is a cleanly, healthy, open-air recreation, devoid of feverish excitements, and yet not destitute of quiet pleasures which are inexpressibly fascinating during the tender years of childhood, and, above all, entirely innocent in their tendencies. As youth succeeds childhood, the love of fishing deepens, and as maturity is attained, this love becomes a part of the man, never to be wholly cast aside. And as old age approaches, and gun and dog and saddle are regretfully retired, angling still remains the contemplative man's pastime. Thus throughout life is angling a source of comfort and pleasure, leaving no bad taste in the mouth or sting in the conscience, and being indeed unequalled by any other sport whatsoever in its purity and guilelessness. For what does Annie Trumbull Slosson's " Fishin' Jimmy" say in his quaint, homely fashion? " I

allers loved fishin', an' know'd 'twas the best
thing in the hull airth. I knows it larnt ye
more about creeters an' yarbs an' stuns an' water
than books could tell ye. I know'd it made folks
patienter and common-senser an'' weather-wiser
an' cuter gen'ally ; gin 'em more fac'lty than all
the school larnin' in creation. I knowed it was
more fillin' than vittles, more rousin' than whiskey,
more soothin' than lodlum. I knowed it cooled
ye off when ye was het, an' het ye when ye was
cold. I knowed all that, o' course, — any fool
knows it. But will ye bleve it ? I was more'n
twenty-one years old, a man growed, 'fore I foun'
out why 'twas that way."

The object of this little book is to explain to
even the youngest reader what " Fishin' Jimmy "
did not find out till he was " a man growed."

I have never had cause to regret that my own
ancestors were professional fishermen, and that I
have been one myself. My father, his father, and
his father, and so on for several more generations,
were watermen and fishermen on the English
Thames. I cannot recollect, therefore, when I
first became an angler ; but like Topsy, " I specs
I grow'd " to be one from the cradle. Self-help

in all pertaining to fishing was, however, the lesson drilled into me from my earliest years, and at an infant's age I first began to handle tackle and tackle-making implements. From *experience*, therefore, I am satisfied that the boy who learns to prepare everything he uses will (as I have done) derive tenfold the pleasure from fishing, that is gotten by the angler who only buys his tackle all ready to his hand. The things that cost pains to procure are the most valued. In the following pages I shall explain the why and wherefore of everything likely to perplex the tyro, as well as the making of each piece of tackling, giving the methods I have myself made use of, with suitable diagrams. Moreover, I shall be pleased at any time to aid my boy-readers by letter, if they write me to my address below.

J. HARRINGTON KEENE.

GREENWICH, Washington County, N.Y.

CONTENTS

PART IV.—WINTER.

PART I

SPRING ANGLING

THE

BOY'S OWN GUIDE TO FISHING

CHAPTER I

SUCKER FISHING

THE earliest fish in the spring of the year to take the bait of the angler, are the trout and the common brook sucker (*Catostomus commersoni*), and the whole family, indeed, of this latter fish; for there are a dozen or more different kinds of suckers. If I were writing for the advanced fisherman, I should begin with the trout; for, with the exception of the head of the family of fishes to which the trout belongs, namely, the salmon, there is no fish pursued by the angler requiring so much care and prudent method for catching. As, however, this is a book for boys, and as the *sucker* is, above all, a boy's fish, and does not require great refinement in tackle to catch, I shall speak at length on it, with the intent that what I shall say will be useful also in the capture of other more difficult fish.

There are, as I have hinted, a dozen or more
species of the sucker in American waters; but the
brook sucker is the one most generally known to
boys, and the ways of *its* capture are suitable for
all the others.   Now, the sucker is an early spring
spawner ; that is, it begins to seek the brooks and
shallow inlets of a river or lake to deposit its eggs
just as soon as the ice begins to go out.   It generally also herds or goes in shoals ; and it is at this
time, whilst the water is still very cold, that the
sucker takes the baited hook most freely, though
it can be caught all the year till the winter ice
and snow shut up the water.   Ordinarily the fish is
snared with a wire or horsehair collar, or speared, or
even netted, being thought of little worth as a food
or sport fish ; but I do not approve of the slaying of
any fish thus unfairly when it is capable of giving
pleasure in its pursuit and capture ; and, therefore,
the way to fish for sucker with hook and line is the
only method that I shall describe in these pages.

It is seasonable to fish for suckers before the
legal season in some States opens for trout, and
even before the leaves begin to appear on the
trees.   It is not necessary to use fine tackle ;
but, of course, if you happen to have a nice rod

and reel, there is no reason why it should not be used. Rods of really good quality can be bought for such a trifle, that most boys will coax a relative to make them a present of one, if they cannot earn the money themselves. However, as self-help is one of the chief charms I have found in fishing, I shall tell you how to equip yourself for sucker fishing at only a few cents' cost.

The ordinary canes that one can buy at the hardware store for a few cents make a capital sucker rod (or even trolling rod for pickerel); but if this is beyond your means, go into the nearest waterside copse, and cut one of the straightest poles you can find. Do this very early in the season, so that you can trim it of all the branches, and set it upright to dry for a little time in the barn. It may be straightened at any specially crooked parts by heating it over the kitchen stove till quite hot, then suspending it from a rafter with a weight — several flatirons will do — to the but, or large end. In a week you will be surprised at the improvement in its appearance. If you want to make it still more useful and neat, go to work as follows: sand-paper off the knots and other irregularities, and, without attempting to remove the bark, apply with a pad several coats of shellac varnish, thinned very thin with alcohol. The pad is made as follows : take a piece of old cotton stocking and wrap it round a ball of batting, making two or three thicknesses of the stocking. Have a wide-mouthed bottle, and place in it one ounce of shellac, filling up with six ounces of alcohol, or even more, to render it a very thin varnish or polish. When you have laid on five or six coats, — drying each one before putting on another, of course, — the polish on your "pole" will be of comparatively elegant appearance.

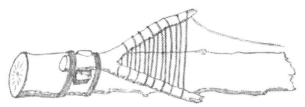

Fig. 1. — Home-made Winder for Pole.

Of course, when the pole assumes this high-toned appearance, you will require a winder for your line. The easiest to make is shown at Fig. 1. It consists of a forked branch, trimmed, and with a notch cut in the end of each leg to hold

the line. To attach it to the rod, you place a
square piece of wood or cork underneath the
lower end, and securely whip or tie it to the
rod-end, as shown. The line is wound in and
out in the outline of a figure 8 round the two
legs of the fork, and stayed at one of the splits
in the ends. Of course, if it is stayed lightly,
any fish requiring loose line can run off the line
at will; though the latter cannot be wound on
again by turning a handle, as in the device that
follows, or in the ordinary brass or wooden reel
sold at the tackle stores.

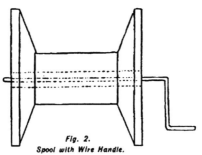

Fig. 2.
Spool with Wire Handle.

A better line-winder, or in this case *reel*, can be
easily made by any boy out of a large thread
spool. In the first place, he must get a length of
moderately thick brass or soft iron wire to form
his handle. This must be bent (Fig. 2) in the

proper form, and passed right through the spool, so that about a quarter-inch projects on the other side. Then it must be plugged or wedged in so that it cannot move; and you have one part of the reel ready. Now go to the tin-shop and get a piece of tin, or copper, or brass, or even sheet-iron, cut in the shape indicated at Fig. 3 ; but be sure it

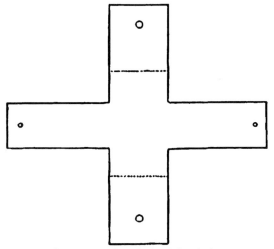

Fig. 3. — Metal Sides for Reel before shaping.

is of the proper size to fit your spool when it is folded at the dotted lines of Fig. 3 and turned up as in Fig. 4. Bore holes in each end of the cross ; place your spool in between the uprights ; screw

the reel on to the rod, and you have quite a sightly
device, as shown at Fig. 5 (p. 18) ; and it will serve

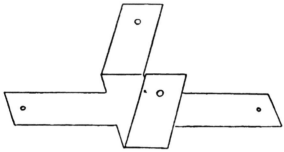

Fig. 4. — Metal Support for Reel.

your purpose for sucker, or even brook-trout worm-
fishing on an emergency, as well as a five-dollar
automatic reel (to which you will be introduced
later on in this work).

You have now the rod and reel ready for work ;
but there is something else to be done to the rod
before the two will work. I refer to the placing
of guides, or rings, through which the line is to
pass. On a ten-foot pole there should be a large
one nearest the reel of not less than half an inch
in diameter ; this may be placed one foot from the
reel. The next three should be placed at equal
distances on the pole, and for the tip a ring of not
less than $\frac{3}{8}$ of an inch inside diameter is best.

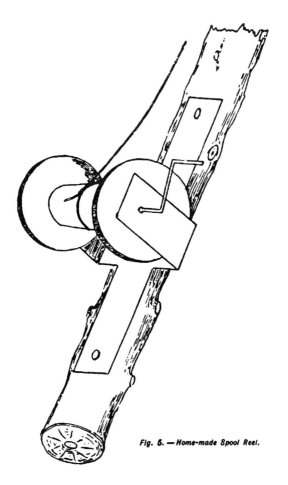

Fig. 5. — *Home-made Spool Reel.*

Now how to make them. Get some medium gauge wire — brass is best, and the gauge should be that of ordinary bell-wire ; take a round stick the diameter you require, and make one turn round it with the wire ; then draw the wire out as if you wished to straighten it, until the ring is like a snake (Fig. 6) ; cut off, and flatten the ends with a

Fig. 6. — Snake Guide.

hammer, or by filing. Thus you have one of the best guides (in principle) it is possible to use. I use no other even on my best rods ; for it is impossible to get the line snarled round it, and there is the minimum of friction to retard its free running. Of course the nearer you get to the top of the rod the smaller should be the ring, though this is not a matter of the first importance. The tip ring is made as shown (Fig. 7), and the two legs are whipped closely on the rod. An easy

Fig. 7. — Home-made Tip Ring.

Fig. 8.—Screw Guide.

rod guide, but not so good a one as that just described, is formed of the little screw picture-frame eyelets sold in the hardware stores (Fig. 8). These may be

screwed into the pole if the wood is hard ; but there
is always a weak spot where they are screwed.   I
prefer at all times the wire guides.

The whipping or binding of the rings requires a
word of explanation.   Fig. 9 shows one of them
as it appears bound on to a pole.   Go to your
shoemaker, and ask him for a piece of his wax
with which he waxes his shoe-thread, and get
some shoe-thread too, or use the spool-thread.
Wax it well, and bind on your rings evenly, as
shown, securing the whipping or binding by
means of two half-hitches (Fig. 9), for I will not

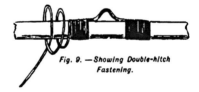

Fig. 9. — *Showing Double-hitch*
Fastening.

now introduce you to the invisible knot ; that will
come later.   Now apply some of your shellac
varnish (with which you varnished your rod) ; and
if you have been careful and neat, you have a ser-
viceable sucker, or bullhead, or " pumpkin-seed "
rod, just as capable of catching these fish as a
more expensive outfit.

The kind of line you will use will depend on

your financial resources, for you cannot make that
at this stage of your angling education. A good
linen line may be bought cheap, and for rough
usage it is to be preferred to the fine silk lines
costing even as high as five cents per yard. The
trouble is that the linen soon soaks up water, and
gets thick and "logy." This, however, may be
remedied in this wise. Wind your line on a card,
not too tightly. Then get an old tomato can or
other receptacle, next some old wax-candle ends
(the paraffine wax is best), and, after cutting out
the pieces of cotton-wick, place them in the can.
Put it on the stove until the wax is quite melted,
but do not get it too hot, or it will burn your line.
Now immerse the line, and keep it in the solution
till thoroughly impregnated. When you think
this is accomplished (and it takes several hours,
according to the thickness of the line), find the
end of the line, still keeping it in the warm solution, and have a companion gently walk back with
it, whilst you pass it through your closed finger
and thumb, to press off the superfluous wax.
This should be done in a warm room, or near the
stove, because the wax cools very rapidly. Having come to the end of your line, stretch it be-

tween two nails, and go over it again with a piece of chamois leather, rubbing hard to engender a little heat, and so render the line smooth. This dressing may be renewed as it seems to wear off, and it will always be found satisfactory for the fishing we are considering.

We now have arrived at the hook. One three-eighths of an inch across the bend is quite large enough for the largest fish. When the fish are plentiful and biting freely you need not trouble about snells, but can use the eyed or ringed hooks.

Fig. 10. — Eyed-hook, with Method of tying.

These are best tied as shown (Fig. 10). Of course the knot there shown is to be drawn tight. But in clear water, and indeed generally, the snelled hook is to be preferred. If you want to do the exactly right thing, send to a tackle dealer and get a "hank" of gut, — which is silk from the silk-worm, taken away before the worm spins it, — and soak it in water. This renders it pliable, so that you can tie a loop at one end like either of the two loops shown (Figs. 11 and 12).   To the other

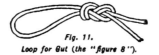

Fig. 11.
Loop for Gut (the "figure 8").

end the hook is whipped, using spool silk, waxed

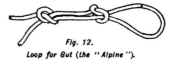

Fig. 12.
Loop for Gut (the "Alpine").

with the shoemaker's wax aforesaid, or with a wax
composed of : —

> Best resin, 2 ounces ; Beeswax, ¼ ounce.

Simmer together ten minutes, and add : —

> Beef tallow, ¼ ounce.

Simmer all together fifteen minutes more, and pour
into a basin of cold water, and pull like candy till
cold and very white.

The whipping or binding of the hook is very

Fig. 13. — Hook whipped, and showing "Invisible Knot."

evenly wound, and secured by means of
the two half-hitches (Fig. 9), or the invisible knot
shown at Fig. 13.   Of course the coils in the
diagram are pulled tight, and the thread drawn

through also as tightly as possible without breaking the thread.   This knot needs practising.

Three strands of horse-hair, preferably from a
gray stallion's tail, will form a good substitute for
the silkworm gut aforesaid ; but it soon wears out,
and is not very strong.

A substitute for a hook can be found in a pin
or needle — the latter is best.   I remember once,
some years back, being near a brook in Vermont
where there were a great number of suckers in
the mill-pool below the dam.   Neither myself nor
friend had any tackle, but we wanted broiled fish
with the other food we had brought.   We turned
out our pockets ; and mine produced a little leather
case of needles and thread (for sewing on buttons,
etc.), and my friend found nothing save the useful

Fig. 14. — Sewing-needle Substitute for Hook.

jackknife.   With this I sent my friend off to cut
a pole ; and selecting a good stout needle, I attached
it in the middle to a double thread of the sewing-
yarn I had with me (Fig. 14).   As will be seen,
the line was attached nearly in the middle of the
needle, and the blunt end was *from*, not *to*, the line.

Presently my companion returned, and we began
hunting for worms. These we found — it being
early spring — near the water, under stones ; and
presently coming upon a good fat one, I thrust
the needle into it as indicated in the diagram (Fig.
15). We had now an ideal bait ; and as I dropped

Fig. 15. — Needle, baited with Worm.

it into the hole where the suckers lay, I knew it
would soon be taken. This proved to be a correct
impression ; but as the worm and needle must be
swallowed, some half-minute was allowed before I
proceeded to strike and draw up. The strike must
be sharp, to draw the *point* of the needle through
the worm's side and catch it on the side of the
fish's throat ; and if it acts successfully, the needle
tears out from the bait and fixes crosswise, so that
it cannot be dislodged, and the fish is then your
meat. It was so in the case I am describing.
We took all we wanted from the pool, and had a
fine "broil" of firm, delicious brook-sucker. "How
did we broil them without utensils ?" you ask.
Well, that did not puzzle us. We whittled out
two thin pine boards, — it was a sawmill where
we encamped, — and stuck them at an angle over

the fire, pinning the suckers, split and cleaned, on them, with a piece of fat pork to each ; and presently they were but a little less toothsome than a trout cooked in the same way.

I have found the needle a good substitute for a hook for eels, their throats being much narrower than other fish ; and with a pair of pincers (pliers) one can take out the needle far easier than the hook from the gullet of these snaky fish.

A sinker and a float, or bob, are desirable for sucker fishing, though not exactly indispensable. The sinker may be of any shape convenient. The most usual is the oblong lead, with an open split ring at each end (Fig. 16) ; but the most convenient

Fig. 16. — Oblong Sinker.

for all styles of fishing where the sinker is needed, is the Tufts " Mackinac " (Fig. 17). As can be seen,

Fig. 17.
" Mackinac Sinker."

it is a shot of different sizes, cut in half, and arranged so that each half screws to the other half.

It can be put on and taken off your line at an instant's notice, and the weight and distance from the hook be varied as you please. Sometimes this is an important point, and may mean all the difference between fish and no fish. A light sinker, not nearer than a foot from the hook, is the best arrangement as a general thing.

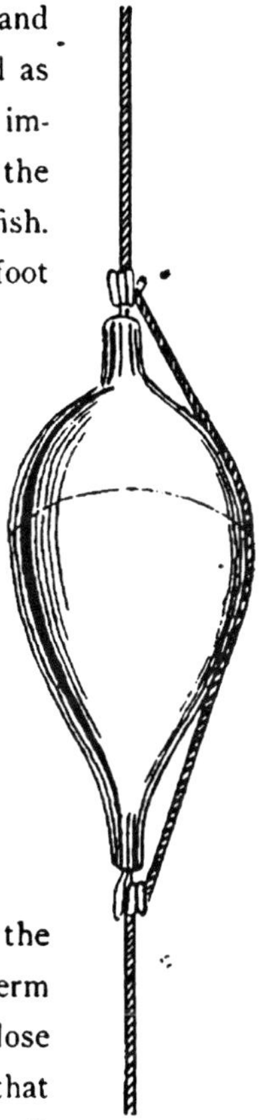

The float, or bob, you can make yourself with the greatest ease. A very simple form is a cork, good and solid, and selected because of its freedom from flaws. This is fashioned like an egg in shape with a jackknife, and a quill may be thrust through it, to which the line is attached. If you choose to make it of wood, choose soft pine, and make it the shape of Fig. 18, filling — as the term is — with oil and whitening, to close up the pores of the wood, and after that either give it a couple of coats of ordinary paint, or varnish it several times

Fig. 18.
Bob, or Float.

with the shellac. The rings (Fig. 18) where the line passes through are made as follows : Twist some rather fine wire three times round a small stick ; cut off both ends at the proper length, one about half an inch and the other flush with the coil. Then turn the coil to right angles, and bind the other ends to the stems of the float, using the silk waxed as before ; touch with shellac varnish, and you have as good a float as you need for sucker fishing. Of course the coiled spring-like arrangement is to allow you to adjust the "bob" to suit any depth of water. The line should be weighted, so that it stands in the water to where the line across is shown in the diagram.

We have now all the tackle necessary, and the next thing is the bait. Nothing beats the garden or earth worm for suckers, and I need not say that it is one of the best of the old "stand-bys" for almost all other kinds of fresh-water fishes. Very few fishes will reject a lively, clean worm, with its pretty tints of coral and pearl and opal iridescence ; that is, it looks like this if you prepare it as I am going to tell you.

"What !" I hear some one exclaim, "fuss with earthworms ! "

"Yes, my young friend," I reply ; "and you will find your basket will take on at least an added twenty per cent per annum in number of fish, if you never fish with worms that have not gone through the preparation I am about to describe."

Dig your worms, in spring, from beneath stones that are near springs that have not frozen ; later you can get them in the garden ; and in summer the smallest you can find by lantern-light from the lawn after a rain at night are good species of earthworm for the angler. The little "gilt cock-spur," as it is called in England, from old rotten manure heaps (it has a yellow tip to its body), and the yellow-banded, bad-smelling "brandling" (it is yellow-banded, — you can't mistake it), are some-times more effectual than the common "gardenia ;" but *all* of them may be gathered as opportunity offers, and constitute eventually valuable bait. Gather your worms in a clean can or other recep-tacle, and place some soil under them, so that they can crawl down through it. Those that have been accidentally bruised, or otherwise hurt, will be too feeble to crawl, and will remain on the top ; and these, together with any dead ones, must be thrown away. Now get a deep earthenware pan or box,

and place a few inches of dampened moss on
the bottom, and turn the worms onto it.   They
will immediately begin to crawl down through, and,
in so doing, will cleanse themselves from all dirt
and impurity.   In a few days, especially if the
moss is washed, and the worms picked over for
lame ones, they will have become almost transpar-
ent, and so tough they cannot be broken by handling or placing them on the hook.   By occasionally
pouring a little sweet milk over them, they can be
kept for a long time ; and a worm so prepared will
live twice as long in the water, and be twice as
lively and attractive, as the worm dug fresh out of
the ground.

I presume it is not necessary for me to tell
my readers *where* to fish for suckers.   Every boy
knows where the fish abound in the spring of
the year, and the brooks where they are most
to be seen.   This axiom stands good for fishing
at all times : " Go where the fish are, — don't
expect them to come to you." It is precisely
because the boy fisherman commonly knows *where*
to fish that he often beats the stranger, wise as
the latter may be in regard to tackle and baits,
and well equipped though he be with all the

Well, having decided to fish in a certain spot, adjust your bob so that the bait will be just off the bottom, and then proceed to bait your hook. Now, there is a right way to do this, and, of course, a wrong; and I want to make the former plain right here, because it is right for trout and bass and other better fish than suckers. Take the hook by the shank between finger and thumb of the right hand, and enter the point into the worm a little distance from the head, so that the head can move when on the hook. Run the hook through to the tail, but not quite out. You now have a *worm-hidden hook*, and both the head and tail are wriggling. The chief advantage, however, is in the fact that you cannot fail to hook the wariest fish if the worm be threaded on in this way. Some prefer looping the worm; but this bunches it, and may and does interfere with the chance of hooking the fish. For bass, the worm is sometimes simply hooked through the middle, and allowed to squirm; and this is very deadly, though an exception to the rule.

The sucker usually goes in herds, and in fishing for him this must be borne in mind. Gently swing out your baited hook, not making more

noise than you can help, and wait patiently, not
running up and down the bank, but at one place,
and quietly watching the bob.   Ha! a tremulous
motion seems to go through it ; now it is still!
again it quivers, and now it slowly disappears.   It
is time to strike, but I beg you to do it swiftly
but not with violence ; and, having hooked the
fish, *don't! don't! don't!* begin to haul in and
try to lift it out by main force.   This is a lesson
you *must* learn in all kinds of fishing, if you would
get the full amount of enjoyment it is able to give.

What you *should* do is as follows (and it applies
to pretty nearly all fish, except the very smallest) :
Strike with a smart twitch, and then, keeping the
point of the rod or pole well up, *first* endeavor to
get your fish out of the immediate neighborhood,
that he may not startle other fish thereabouts ;
and next tire him so that he comes ashore readily,
putting, all the while, the strain on the elastic
pole.   If you do this, you will seldom break loose
from the fish or break your tackle ; but if you
follow your first impulse, and attempt to "yank"
the sucker out, you may break your rod or line,
especially if the fish is a large one (and I have
caught them up to four pounds).

I have thoroughly enjoyed sucker fishing, and so may my readers. In the spring, whilst the snow-water yet runs down from the mountains, the fish are gamey, and fight with a good deal of bull-dog like courage. Moreover, they are quite palatable to eat ; and that my boy readers may know how to clean and prepare the fish for cooking, the following few words of experience will be in order.

Kill your fish by means of a stone or stick, striking it on the back of the head. If it is a small one, you can place your thumb into its mouth, — its soft mouth cannot hurt you, — and, pressing the ball of the thumb against the roof of the mouth and the finger on the head outside, quickly jerk the head back. This will break the neck, and death is instantaneous. Kill all fish at once after catching them : it is merciful to do so (and " blessed are the merciful ").

When you get home, whilst the fish is still fresh and moist, plunge it into *scalding* water (two parts boiling, one part cold), and after letting it remain a few seconds, withdraw it, and see if the scales come off easily ; if not, give it rather more time in the hot water. When the scales come off very readily, as they will do when scalded sufficiently, scrape them carefully off, and cut off the fins with an old pair of shears. Wipe off all the slime and coloring matter of the fish; and it should be snow-white when properly done. Do not place it in water of any kind again, but when you cut it open, use a damp towel to cleanse the interior parts. Cut off the head; and if it is early in the season you have a firm, palatable fish.

There is no better way to cook this fish than by broiling, or frying it in pork-fat. The latter should be very hot, and the fish should be cut in pieces of suitable length. It is to be eaten with a plain boiled potato, and a squeeze of lemon-juice over the fish; and the boy must be an epicure indeed who cannot enjoy it. If the fish be a large one, say over two pounds, the backbone may be taken out by opening it carefully down the back and cutting away the flesh from each side, using a long, thin, and flexible knife for the purpose. My readers should practise fish dissection in this way. Last summer I astonished some unbelieving friends by taking out every bone of a large shad they brought to me, and I did not cut away much meat either. But to return to our

sucker fishing. I have found the fishing best
when the wind has been in the south or south-
west; and on the best day last year I caught
seven, averaging two pounds apiece, in two hours.
These were as many as I wanted; and, like good
old Izaak Walton, I required them only to give to
a "poor body" with a large family, so I consider
it was very good luck. As I used much finer
tackle than was suggested in the foregoing, I had
the greater sport; but there is no reason why my
boy friends may not do likewise with their own
tackle, as here described.

CHAPTER II

PICKEREL TROLLING IN SPRING

As soon as the ice goes out of the lakes where pickerel (*Esox lucius*) abound, some grand sport may be had trolling. There is a fitness also in referring to this form of pike-fishing at this place, because I want this little book to be progressive, and we take one step higher in fishing for pickerel than in fishing for suckers. The trout season opens, it is true, near about this time in the spring; but it will be well for you to come with me, bringing your coarse tackle, for one day before you essay to catch the beautiful "salmon of the fountains," which is what is meant by the scientific name of the brook-trout (*Salmo fontinalis.*)

A pole is not actually necessary in trolling, though, for my own part, I always use one. Two lines may be used; and there should be two of you in the boat, — one to row, and the other to manipulate the lines. These should be of linen, eight

braid, and very strong, and dressed with the par-
raffine wax dressing before given. One hundred
and fifty feet is not too much line for each, and
a winder (Fig. 19) can be made out of soft wood

Fig. 19. — Winder for Trolling-line, etc.

to contain each one (though be sure to unwind
and dry them after reaching home at night). In
order to render the allure more likely to attract
fish by reason of its connection with the line
being less visible, I always attach three feet
of three-ply twisted fine brass wire to the line,
taking care to have a large swivel — duly tested
to see that it is strong at each end (Fig. 20).

Fig. 20. — Swivel.

Through the swivel at the line end goes the line ;
and through that at the other end goes the allure,
be it spoon, or artificial fish, or large trolling-fly,
or dead fish.

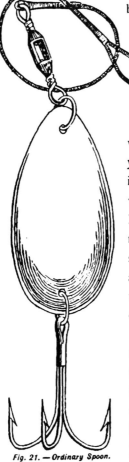

Fig. 21. — *Ordinary Spoon.*

Without doubt the spoon-bait (Fig. 21) is the best all round allure for trolling for pickerel in the spring of the year. Fig. 22 is one of Chapman's make of Clayton, N.Y.; and with one like this he last year caught a mascalonge in the River St. Lawrence weighing forty-two pounds. But the ingenious boy can make a spoon that will serve his purpose almost as well, though of course it will not appear so finished or handsome.

In the first place, he must coax his good mother to let him have an old teaspoon, plated is good enough (silver is too good to lose), and cut off the bowl just above where the handle

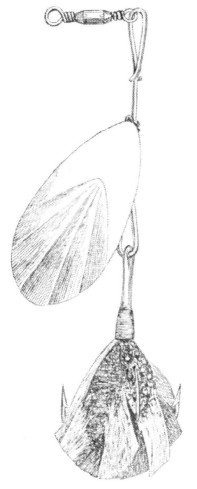

Fig. 22. ----- Chapman Spoon.

sets in with a file. Having done this neatly, he must
bore a hole in each end, and be careful that the
edges of the hole are rounded and smooth, or
they may cut the whipping of his hooks. He
now has a spoon bowl with two holes in it; the
smaller end we will call the top, and the larger
end the bottom. Now, the smaller end _must_ be
the one next nearest the trolling-line, or the spoon
won't spin; and into the hole he passes a small
strong split ring, to be got at any hardware store.
Keeping it open with his knife, he now slides the
ring of the swivel, to which he has attached a
length of gimp guitar-string, and a ringed triplet
hook is placed in the lower hole, also by means of
a split ring. The lure now looks like Fig. 21, and
will catch fish as it is; but it is better to tie some
gaudy feathers on the shank of the lower hook, to
hide the very "rank" barbs (Fig. 22). The tying
of these feathers need not be difficult, and almost
any bright feathers, begged from your sister's hat,
will do. Tie them, as recommended in sucker
fishing for the whipping of hooks, and you now
have a lure just as likely to catch a forty-two
pound mascalonge as Mr. Chapman's beautiful
weapon shown in Fig. 22.

Curiously enough, it is not always the most elegant spoon that catches most fish ; though what I am going to relate by no means should be used as an argument against nice tackle, but rather as an apology for the inferior kind. Some years ago I was living on the shore of Lake Cossayuna, Washington County, N.Y., and near by me lived my friend, Wm. McClellan, also a most devoted disciple of Izaak Walton. One day in early spring he sought me out, and prevailed on me to take another with us to row, and to go a-

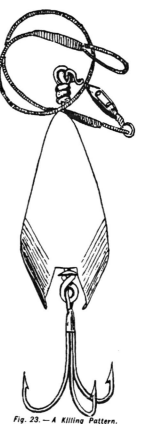

Fig. 23. — A Killing Pattern.

trolling. Said I, " William, I must rig me out a spoon with fine feathers, and new hooks, for this auspicious occasion. See, I have one of friend Chap-

man's finest (see Fig. 22), and the hooks are as
vivid as Jacob's coat of many colors." — " Bosh,"
said he, " this is good enough for me ;" and he
called attention to a blurred and battered and
rusted old *tin* spoon, to which some colorless
threads of feathers hung in scarecrow fashion ;
" and what is more, it will catch twice as many
as your brand new tackling, I'll wager." — " Ha,
ha !" I roared, " hang it up in the apple-tree for
the birds to laugh at, but don't disgrace me with
such a spoon-bait." But fish with it he would and
did. We rowed back and forth on the lake all
that morning, and caught thirty-seven pickerel ;
and how many do you suppose fell to the share
of my splendid spoon-bait ? Just *four.* I tried
everything to change the luck. I even fished
right in my friend's water, with my bait revolving
only a few inches away from his ragged old bait ;
and even then the fish preferred his lure to mine.
Oh, how he did tease about it ! I never met him
but he reminded me of this, the only occasion
when I was badly beaten by him. I made it up
next day. Now, I grieve to say, he is dead —
gone to that " undiscovered country from whose
bourn no traveller returns." (Rest in peace !)

Other shapes of allures are sometimes very successful in trolling. Fig. 23 shows a shape that can be cut out of tin, and will serve, though of course nothing beats the spoon amongst the fancy baits. I have sometimes made a rough-and-ready arrangement answer admirably, as I did once last spring. It was this way. I was passing by a famous hole in the river near where I live, and in the bright warm beams I saw a four to five pound pickerel basking near the shore. How to capture him I had not the least idea; but I sat down on a stone and began a search in my pockets. Item 1, a pair of nail shears, small, but strong; item 2, a piece of silk fish-line about four yards long, and strong; item 3, a jackknife; item 4, some pieces of lead; item 5, an eel-hook, large, and ringed at end of shank. This is what I did. I cut a pole and tied my line securely to it; next I looked around, and, this being a well-known sucker pool, I found an old tin worm-box. With the shears (I confess I spoiled them), I cut a piece of tin in the shape of a fish, roughly fashioned, of course; and with one of the points I bored a hole in both ends of the bait. In one hole I slipped the ring of the hook, and closed it tight

by hammering with a stone; in the other I tied
the line two or three times through, so that it
would be less likely to be cut, and lo and
behold! I had a glittering pickerel bait. With
my heart beating loudly, I approached the water,
and looked over to where my pickerel had lain.
He wasn't there!   Oh, the throes of disappoint-
ment I experienced after all my trouble!   I
was on the verge of throwing the whole thing
into the stream, and telling him to take it when
he next came that way, when, on peering closely
again, I caught sight of the cold, malicious, fierce
eye of this river pirate from beneath a patch of
weeds near where I first saw him; and in a moment I dropped the glistening bait, not in front
of him, for that would have scared him, but just
behind, drawing it slowly away.   In a second he
was on it, with a ferocious rush and a tremendous
splash, and I felt at once he had hooked himself.
I dared not be severe with him, and you may
imagine the tussle I had with no reel and only
four yards or so of line.   Backwards and forwards
he struggled, and I saw that he was securely
hooked in the fleshy part of the mustache or
movable lip; and by and by, to shorten my story,

I drew him to shore, and, stooping and putting my finger and thumb in his eyes, threw him well upon the bank. (This is the best way to land a pickerel if you had no landing-net.)

Trolling for pickerel with the Caledonian minnow is another good way (Fig. 24), and trolling with a large hook to which white feathers have been tied somewhat in the form of a fish, occasionally is productive of a good basket ; but, next to the spoon, the dead natural bait certainly takes precedence of all.

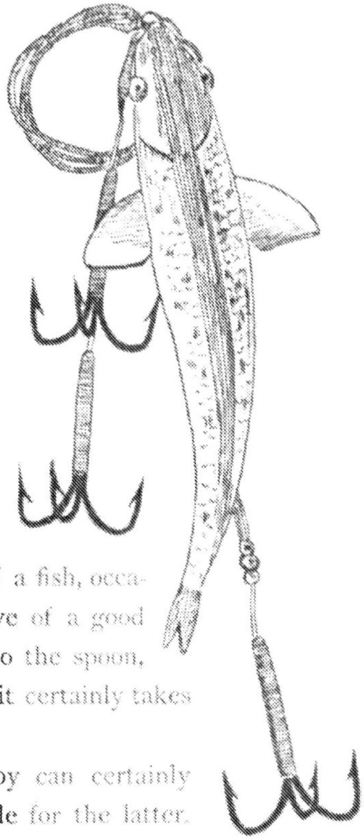

An ingenious boy can certainly make his own tackle for the latter. That which I prefer is shown Fig. 25, and consists of a piece of rather

Fig. 24.
Caledonian Minnow.

stout sheet copper cut with the shears to the form
of Fig. 25 at A.   The hooks are attached as also
shown.   To bait it the shaft (Fig. 25, A) is thrust
down the throat of the dead bait, and the tail of
the bait bent to a sufficient curve to cause it to
spin, or rather to gyrate, with a sort of "wabble,"
which is very attractive to pickerel.   The hooks
lie alongside the bait.   It is seldom on a bright
day, with the wind not too cold, that the tyro
cannot capture pike with one or the other of the
lures I have described.   I have also found the fin
of a perch, or the belly part of a small pickerel, an
excellent substitute for the spoon.

Great Lake Trout (the *Salmo namaycush*) are
also caught by trolling in a somewhat similar way,
and at about the same time of the year ; but as it is
not likely my boy readers will take up Great Lake
trolling at this stage of the subject, I will not do
more than mention the fact that on Lake George
the experts use a gang, whereon the bait-fish is
impaled.   The one described above will do very
well ; and having out a long, strong line, they
travel for miles, trolling this bait behind the boat,
and their patience is rewarded with great fish,
ranging up as high as the twenties, and even
higher.   (This is true of the West especially.)

Fig. 26. — Home-made Gang.

Then, again, the mascalonge is taken this way ;
but though trolling for this fish is at best very
elementary angling, it is not to be expected that
boys will want to undertake it until they have mastered the rudiments of the finer and more scientific angling for smaller and more manageable
fishes.

The best time in the North for pickerel trolling
on the lakes and rivers is when the apple-trees are
in full blossom ; but the fish can be caught much
earlier, and I have referred to it in the present
order of sequence as a spring pastime, because
considerable and undivided attention must be
given to the next chapter.   Moreover, I wanted to
lead my pupils up to trout fishing by stepping-
stones to knowledge, as it were.

Two useful implements must not be forgotten
when one goes trolling ; viz., the disgorger and the
home-made rack for keeping open the fish's mouth.
As you know, the pickerel has long and sharp
teeth, and one is very apt to get a nasty bite or
cut when unhooking the fish, if not in some way
protected.   The device I use is a V-shaped or
forked piece of stout wood or bifurcated branch.
It is cut from a bush of any stiff wood.   To use it,

the apex or small end of the V is pushed into the pickerel's mouth sidewise, and turned round, open-ing the jaw, and thus keeping them open. The disgorger is simply a stick with a V-shaped piece cut out of the end, and may be also made either of bone or hard wood or metal. To use it, take the line in the left hand and pass the notch into the bend of the hook, and the latter is then readily dislodged.

CHAPTER III

BAIT-FISHING FOR TROUT

As soon as the trout fishing opens, this beautiful game fish will readily take the worm ; indeed, it is not at all uncommon to get a trout when sucker fishing, but they are then not yet in good condition, and take the bait with hesitation, and show no fighting power or resistance. Indeed, so late as the 1st of May in 1893 I have found them "logy" and sucker-like in Vermont (Bennington County) ; and many times when I pulled up a trout I could have made an affidavit, before seeing the fish, that it was a sucker from the tameness of its behavior ; indeed, the suckers bit with greater freedom, and caused more exertion of skill to land them with fine tackle than the trout.

But what a fine basket of fish myself and friend did catch on that same May 1, 1893 ! We drove all night from Greenwich, N.Y., nearly twenty miles, up hill and down, and in a blinding rain-storm. By daylight we were at the brush factory,

West Arlington, Vermont; and as we took our horse out of the buggy, we found we were not alone, but several other kindred souls, including a lady and a little girl, were ready to begin fishing also. All the few inhabitants of the village turn out on May Day to fish the lovely Ondawa; for that is the first day of the season, and the first fishing after the long Vermont winter. But on this occasion it rained, and rained, and rained! and yet through it all we caught half-pounders and less-sized fish, till our baskets were full to overflowing; and then, while yet midday, we had dinner at our friend Babcock's, — the redoubtable and evergreen Jim Babcock, may his shadow never grow less, — and came away.

Fishing with the bait is greatly practised in mountain streams all the trout year, but there are special features attending it in the springtime that do not appear in the later season. The fish, as the weather becomes warm, are getting hungry after their long winter's fast, and seize the bait greedily; and very soon one finds that to make a good basket it is necessary to use much strategy; for the trout, unlike the sucker, is easily scared.

Oh, how glorious it is to follow some purling

stream down in these halcyon spring days! and, whilst the birds and flowers and greening hills are manifest to your appreciative senses, to catch this beautiful Apollo of the stream with deft and careful skill! How the season, the beauty of nature, and the invigorating atmosphere and sunshine combine to make a setting for this best of spring fishing! I beg of you, boys, not to miss it. Many springs have I pursued it, and never once has it disappointed me.

But you must be told the best way to go about it. And, first, the rod must be considered anew. I really think, by this time, — by the time our young angler has got to the dignity of trout-fishing, — it is right he discarded the copse-cut pole and arrived at a real rod. Not that the *pole* will not catch fish, but there is additional pleasure to be gotten out of the use of nicer and finer tackle. The pole does well enough for primitive spots yet existing, and for the olden times, when only the lazy boys of the village seemed to do the fishing; but now, when young gentlemen, in the intervals of their studies, go angling, and when even the fish have grown educated, it is time to make use of what Mr. Gladstone calls the " re-

sources of civilization;" and I therefore insist on
a real rod, line, reel, and leader for spring trout
fishing.

The rod. If you can afford it, go to your nearest drug-store, and you can get a jointed 12-foot
bamboo for about one dollar. This is quite good

Fig. 26. — Cheap Brass Reel.

enough for brook bait-fishing, and if you break it
going through the brush it is no great matter. I
myself sometimes use to this day such a rod, and
find it both light and convenient. A plain brass
reel will serve, something after the pattern shown
at Fig. 26, and a silk line of 75 feet is long enough

for all brook purposes. It should not be too thick, and may be dressed in the wax referred to on an earlier page. Of course, the rod must be supplied with guides.

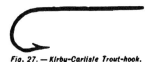

Fig. 27. — Kirby-Carlisle Trout-hook.

The best hook I know for bait-fishing for trout is the eyed Pennell hook (Fig. 10) ; but a round bend hook, not more than three-eighths inch across the bend, is suitable. It must have a long shank ; and the kind I like best is that known as the Kirby-Carlisle (Fig. 27). This has a slight side twist, and this twist enables the hook to hook into the fish more quickly than would otherwise be the case.

Fig. 28. — Hook for Worm-fishing with Bristle Attachment.

Of course gut is used for the snell ; and, at the same time the hook is bound on, a short piece of thin wire or gut or bristle is tied alongside it, so that it projects one-quarter of an inch above the end of the shank (Fig. 28). This prevents the bait from slipping down and becoming a bunch on the hook. It is properly baited by running the hook through from head to tail.

Sometimes a little float, or bob, of white quill is useful to let you know where your line is, and to indicate the least bite. I often use a piece of cork about the size of a bean to carry the line down and indicate its whereabouts. Of this, however, more later.

Fig. 29. — Basket or Creel.

We will now suppose the angler arrived at the stream. He needs to have a bag or basket to contain his fish and lunch, and we will spend a moment in considering this useful piece of equipment. Now, the ordinary form of basket is shown in Fig. 29, and answers very well. I have no fault

to find with it ; but it costs a dollar or more, and a
bag made of an old linen sheet or table-cloth,
which can be washed every time after being used,
is even preferable.   I object to putting my fresh
and beautiful trout into an ill-smelling basket ; and
it is almost impossible to deodorize or get out the
smell of fish if once it has got well into the porous
woodwork.   Then, again, the basket soon rots, —

Fig. 30. — Home-made Fish-bag.

about three seasons is the life of it, — and you
have to buy another.

A bag something like Fig. 30 is the most suitable for the boy bait trout-fisher.   He can also carry
his worms in the small bag at *a*, Fig. 30, in damp
moss, and thus avoid the extra trouble of attaching
a tin bait-box.   However, if he wishes to do this,
Fig. 31 is a good pattern.   My own bag is a leath-
ern one, and so made that it can be turned inside

out to be scrubbed ; and a little leather pouch no larger than a cigar-case carries all my fishing tackle when out bait-fishing. Of course fly-fishing is another story, and we shall have a great deal to consider beyond the foregoing when we come to that fine art of angling.

Fig. 31.—*Tin Worm-box, with Safety-pin Attachment.*

Now, in fishing in a stream, no matter how large or how small it may be, here are some maxims you must bear in mind :—

Don't get nearer the water than you are absolutely obliged. Reach as far as possible with your rod.

Don't go stamping around as if you were cold. Tread lightly ; trout can hear by means of the nervous apparatus attached to each scale (you didn't know trout had scales ! Well, they certainly have !) ; and they feel, if they don't hear, as you do, the tread of the heavy-footed angler.

Don't fish *down* stream in slow flowing water, but up.   If the water is swift, you *must* fish down.

Don't yank your fish out of the water as if you wanted him to fly, but it is well to get him out with reasonable haste.

Don't fish hastily ; *don't* be afraid to renew your bait frequently ; and *don't* forget that the most successful fisherman is he who has his line the most in the water.

With these few *don'ts* as preliminary to the lesson, I now proceed to fish a typical mountain brook with you.

Of course your worms are well scoured, as I told you in the chapter on sucker fishing.   That being so, select a moderately large one, and bait your hook.   Here the stream runs through grass land tolerably level.   Crawl near and let your bait fall gently.   It is invariably as soon as the bait touches the water that the voracious little fish bite — and ha! you have one, but it is very small, too small to keep.   Yes, the State enacts five inches as the least size at which the trout may be kept ; and taking your little fish off as gently as possible, we throw him back.   Try down by yonder bush that hangs over the stream ; drop your line in so that the current carries the bait towards the roots of the alder. Now watch it in its course. It rolls gently and slowly down stream ; and, as it nears the largest root, there is the flash of a fish swifter than that of the lightning, if it be possible, and the bait is seized. Don't hesitate — strike ! There you have him ! and the next moment he swings out in the air a good quarter-pounder. Do you wish to preserve the coloring of this very handsome specimen to show the folks at home ? Well, kill the fish as I instructed you when speaking of sucker fishing, by pressing the ball of the thumb against the roof of its mouth, and snapping the vertebra ; and here is a piece of fine tissue paper. Always carry some with you ; it occupies but little space in your pocket, and if it be closely wrapped round a trout, will cling by reason of the natural moisture of the fish so tight as to exclude all air and most of the light ; and so you will find when you get home and wash it off, your fish is as bright spotted and handsome as when it first came from the stream.

Fish carefully, especially in the spring, all the shallows, and most carefully those near to holes and trouty nooks. After the spawning season the fish retire to the deeper water, wherever they can find it, for the winter, and emerge in spring to seek food and to increase their muscular strength by engaging with the swifter currents of the runlet. Ah, here we arrive at a piece of thick alder swamp which almost hides the brook. Shall you fish it? Why, certainly. It may be almost impossible to reach every likely looking spot, but you must by no means pass this by. Right down between these branches lies a trout for sure. Take your rod, patiently shorten the line by winding in till only a yard remains free from the tip; now roll the rod round, and so wind up the line on the tip till you can pass it and the baited hook through the matted branches. Now carefully turn your rod the reverse way; that is, unwind the line on the tip, and, being very expectant, drop it gently near that cavernous root. Ha, another! don't give any line at all. He is the best fish of all; simply hold your rod point up, and let him kick. Your tackle will stand it. Now draw him through as you best can; and to do it you must, I fear, spoil your chances of another fish, because of your eager trampling to get your half-pound trout. Well, there is always, even with old anglers, a first day's

excitability of nerves; and the next time you get a
fish in just this way, you will probably basket him
without scaring the others sure to be in the pool
also.   Remember this, and it is one of the axioms,
— the best fish are in the best places, and where
there is one good, i.e., large, fish, there is likely to
be more.

Now, in the next meadow is a corduroy cart-
bridge, and beneath it there is sure to be fish of
some kind, — small, medium, or large, and perhaps
all three.   Put on another worm, and let us try it.
What, you can't get the old one off because of the
bristle at the top of the hook?   Pull it right up
on to the gut-snell, then; now double the snell, and
draw the worm through the closed thumb and
finger.   That gets it off, doesn't it?   There are
more ways of killing a cat than by simply hanging
it, you know.   Here's our cart-bridge, and we stand
a rod or more above it.   Now crawl to a firm spot
on the bank about twelve feet away from it, and
draw out about fifteen feet of your line, so that
you may reach some three feet under it with your
bait.   How are you going to get your bait there?
Wait a bit; I'll show you.   Here is a flat chip of
wood about as big as the palm of your hand.   I lay

it down, and, putting the baited hook on it near
the middle, I coil the line in loose coils around on
the chip. Now launch it on the stream, so that it
floats down the middle ; hold up your rod, and guide
it, which you can easily do as the line uncoils.
Be alert ; it is getting near the end of the tether :
for at once, as the chip passes from under the bait
and it falls on the water, I expect that you will
get a bite. You cannot see the chip or bait, but
— hurrah, you can feel the hooked fish ! Draw
him up quickly ; he is not the largest to be found
there. Search for another chip, and by the time it
is all arranged there will be yet a bigger trout
waiting. In summer a leaf is as good as a chip of
wood, and sometimes neither is needed, and a
piece of quill or white stick of wood will act quite
well as a float, or bob, to carry your bait to the spot
you are aiming at.

If you are fishing a brook such as the one we
have been "supposin'," and have a friend with
you, you must not have him alongside you, or
even within talking distance, as I have been ; but
if possible, one fish up and the other down, both
returning to meet at the point from whence you
started. If, however, you want to fish down, pull

straws to see which one shall start first; and if
you lose, sit patiently down till your friend has
got at least fifteen minutes' start. These fifteen
minutes allow the fish to settle again, and is little
enough. I prefer half an hour on much-fished
streams. Then go to work, and fish slowly, and
do not miss any spot because it is difficult.

If you have to fish *up* stream, additional care
must be exercised to approach the water quietly,
— and don't fall into the error which nearly every
novice seems to be unable to avoid; namely, that
of walking a piece and then fishing *down*. Cast
your bait with a swinging motion *up* always, and
you will find quite as many, and possibly more,
taken than if you used a long line *down*. In up-
stream, and sometimes in down-stream, fishing,
especially if the wind be blowing so as to carry
your line away from where you want it to go, it
is necessary at times to use a sinker. In that
case a No. 1 shot split will be ordinarily sufficient. It should be pinched on at a foot from the
bait.

In worm-bait fishing in large waters — rivers
or wide brooks — where large fish exist, a *double*
hook tackle is sometimes used; with this the bait

can be cast somewhat as the artificial fly ; and it
is a very sure hooking arrangement, but it is not
necessary for general use unless the trout run
large.   Ordinarily the medium-sized long-shanked
Kirby-Carlisle hook is most suitable.

Other natural baits may often be used with
success in trout fishing in spring if they do not
seem to care for the worm ; though at this season
the worm is far and away the best bait, and can
always be got by the waterside if you run short
of your cleansed garden worms.   In some streams
the fresh-water shrimp is to be found, and *two*
should be impaled on a rather smaller hook than
that in use for worm-fishing.   You will find them
under stones.   Then, there is the larvæ of the
stone flies or the case or caddis insects.   You
take one of these and squeeze it, and instantly the
little black head of the creature pops out of the
case in which it dwells.   The latter looks exactly
like a bit of twig or stick on the gravel, and its
dress shows another of nature's benevolent ways
of hiding its creatures from observation by making them precisely like their surroundings.   The
grub or worm out of its case is like a maggot, and
is a most killing lure.   Every brook, it is true,

does not possess this larvæ, but most waters containing trout do so. It is, at any rate, well to search for them if the fish are known to be plenty and are not biting at the worm.

I have caught trout with other lures odder than these. Once up in the wilds of New Brunswick, Canada, whilst camping with a friend on the Magaguadavic River (pronounced Magádavick), our guide surprised us by thus commenting on the big one and two pound trout we were frying for supper : " These trout ain't no use fer eating ; I'd sooner hev corned beef," — we thought them (and they *were*) most palatable, — " but I'll take yer to-morrow where the trout ain't larger than herrings, and black as yer hat, and they won't take nuthin' but bits of chubs fer bait." I stared at Davis incredulously ; but he was serious, and on the morrow it proved as he had said. The water where they lived proved to be a sluggish, almost dead little slough, or " sloo," running out of a swamp thick with moss and decaying vegetation, and the water was of India-ink blackness (of a deep rich brown black), and we used just such tackle as I have been describing, baited with pieces of chub, or even pieces of their brothers

and sisters, as we discovered when our supply of
chubs ran out. They were black all over, except
on the belly, which was silvery white ; and on the
dark sides could be faintly seen the customary
red spots, only they were of the deepest blood-
crimson color. The largest we caught was not
one-quarter of a pound, and I think we must have
taken a hundred out of a space of water not four
yards square.

 I do not recommend the use of pieces of fish
for brook-trout in this country, but I have re-
peatedly caught them with the light belly fin, and
with the eye from another fish.

In late spring, when the water begins to clear
and become low, and the sunny days return,
maggot-bait fishing is sometimes most effective,
and it may be practised at all times through the
summer when the water is low and the weather
too warm for worm-fishing to be of any use.
Any boy can breed the maggots without the
process being offensive, if he will follow out the
following instructions : Obtain a beef's liver from
the butcher, and slash it with a knife in half a
dozen places; put it into an old tin pail free
from holes, and cover it with a lid so arranged

that the parent blow-flies or blue-bottles can get *in*, but that no cat can get the liver out. Let it remain in the sun until it has been very freely "blown;" then remove it to a shady spot, and cover it up from the rain or other disturbing influence. In a few days more or less, according to the weather, the eggs will hatch, and the young maggots will begin to feed and grow. In a week they will be full-grown, and the liver all eaten, or nearly so. You must now, with a forked stick, lift out what remains of this, and bury it; and then turn your maggots out into an earthen pan or jar half filled with dry mould and sand. Place them in the cellar for coolness — there is now nothing offensive in them — for twenty-four hours, and then turn them into fresh bran. In a few hours they will be white as ivory, and a most tempting bait for trout. It is a good plan to throw in a few every now and then in advance of you as you walk down the stream. They should be placed on the hook as in Fig. 32 (p. 68).

Brook fishing with bait is the best apprenticeship possible for the young angler, and it may be extended to river and lakes with ever-increasing confidence. Grasshopper fishing for the same fish

comes later in the year, and will be referred to at
the appropriate time.

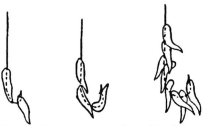

Fig. 32. — Maggots baited according to Size of Hook.

Let the young fisherman never forget that fine
and far off — which means light fine tackle, and
fishing as far away from the fish as possible —
is a secret as well worth practising to-day as in
Walton's time, — two hundred and more years
ago, when the axiom was first put in print.

PART II

SUMMER ANGLING

CHAPTER IV

FISHING FOR THE SUN-FISH AND OTHER "BOYS' FISHES"

DISTINCTIVELY a boys' fish is the sun-fish, or "pumpkin-seed;" and when the other game fishes, trout, bass, etc., are no longer plentiful, this despised little gamin amongst fishes will be as highly esteemed by anglers as are some of the "coarse" fishes by Englishmen over the water. Everybody knows the sun-fish, bold in biting, and fearlessly fighting to the last on the hook. On fine tackle they give quite good sport; and I have frequently quit fishing for the large-mouthed black bass and pickerel in some warm-water lake in summer, because I preferred taking the bold-biting and voracious sun-fish.

The food of these little fish consists of the crustacea and larvæ of the water, and they will take almost anything a trout will feed on. Worms, maggots, dobsons, grasshoppers, and crickets are their favorite baits; and as these are easily pro-

curable, the boy angler has
no difficulty in providing a
good string of sun-fish if he
knows ever so little how to
fish.   They will also take
the artificial fly ; and much
fun have I had with them
with the " brown hackle,"
which will be described farther on.

The tackle most suitable
for these small fry is a light bamboo cane pole, jointed if you like
and can afford it ; and if not, in
one length of about ten feet,
with guides and a reel, as directed for trout.   Let your line be
a fine one, dressed as for trout,
and do not omit to have a yard
of medium fine gut for leader.
Also snell your hook, which should
be a No. 5 (Fig. 33) on moderately fine gut ; for though the
sun-fish is a bold biter, you will
find that you catch two fish with

fine tackle, where only one will respond to the "pole and cord" style of equipment.

In sun-fish angling I always use a float, or bob; and a very good one for this purpose can be made of a turkey quill feather, as I directed you when speaking of *sucker* fishing. Split shot should be closed on the leader, to sink the float so that three-quarters of an inch rises above the surface of the water; and so adjusted as to lift the bait about six inches from the bottom of the water. You are then in a fair way to catch fish.

By the way, there is a rough-and-ready way to split your shot I don't think I told you of. Get out your jackknife, make a slight circular indentation in a piece of hard wood, — the top of a post will do, — lay the shot in this, and simply cut the lead halfway through. All sizes of shot, from buck-shot to No. 5's, should be split and kept ready in a pill-box; and the preparation of these is a good job for a rainy afternoon.

Having selected the spot you intend to fish, be quiet; for though these fish are not easily scared, you want to be light, and not boisterous, in your movements. Bait the hook with a small wriggling

worm or grasshopper, or either of the other bait
I mentioned, and gently swing it out. Presently
you will see by the tremulous motion of the bob
that a sun-fish is biting — then down it goes beneath the surface. A sharp strike fixes the hook
firmly; and now you have quite a fight on hand
before the plucky little fellow gives up. Size for
size, he is little inferior to the trout in this respect,
though I am aware "comparisons are odorous," as
Mrs. Malaprop would say. A very good variation
of the tackle is thus made. Place the split shot
or sinkers (sufficient, of course, to "cock" the
float or bob) at the end of the leader. Now tie
one of the snelled hooks at a distance of six inches
above the sinker, at right angles, and above this,
at a distance of another six inches, tie on another
hook. You can thus use two kinds of bait, and
frequently catch two fish at a time. Should you
get two half-pounders hooked, you have got a con-
test indeed that will occupy all your wits and resources for a few minutes. Especially as I urgently
insist you must not lift the fish from the water
until they have had their struggle out. Of course
if you, on the other hand, insist on doing so, you
must use very strong tackle, or be broken unex-

pectedly at some odd time when a larger and stronger fish is visiting you.

The sun-fish has a bad habit of stripping the worm from the hook. I know of no cure for this ; but if you watch carefully, and learn their methods of biting, you will soon be able to time your strike so that this does not happen once in ten bites.

These little fish are very good pan fish in early summer, but become " wormy " as the water gets warmer. The black spots with which they are then sometimes covered is caused by the cyst or cell of a minute " worm " or larvæ parasite. Do you not remember that : —

> " Big fleas have little fleas
> Upon their backs to bite 'em,
> And little fleas have lesser fleas,
> And so on *ad infinitum !* "

Under the heading of sun-fish there are many members of the family, all to be taken as I have described, or to be gotten with the artificial fly. I do not go into detail anent the fly at this time, as that branch of fishing will be dealt with exhaustively when I come to hold forth on trout fly-fishing ; and any one who can catch trout with the fly can of a surety catch "pumpkin-seeds" by the same method.

The other members of the sun-fish family, besides the well-known *Lepomis gibbosus*, are the long-eared sun-fish (*L. megalotis*), known throughout the Mississippi Valley and south-westward to the Rio Grande, and in the north-west, and plentiful in Indiana and Illinois; the yellow belly, or bream (*L. auritus*), found plentifully east of the Alleghanies from Maine to Florida, and also in Virginia and the Carolinas; the blue gill (*L. pallidus*), the most widely diffused of all; the green sun-fish (*L. cyanellus*), found in all waters between the Rocky Mountains and the Alleghanies, and several more not necessary to be specially enumerated. They are all to be caught with the angle-worm, and are all "boys' fishes."

One step above the sun-fishes, towards the game fish properly so called, we find the rock bass (or red eye). This fish is fond of quiet, rocky pools, and is a fiercely preying and pluckily fighting member of the great bass family. He takes almost everything, from a piece of raw meat to a black beetle, and is best caught with rather larger hooks and stronger tackle than his brother the sun-fish. The same remark applies to the "crappie," so beloved of the youth of the Mississippi Valley. Small fish are a good bait for these, and also for the rock bass ; and I have caught the latter in great plenty in the upper Hudson on "dobsons," — the larvæ of the *corydalus cornutus*, or helgramite fly.

To fish for the yellow perch is yet one step higher in angling promotion, and very nearly approaches the art of catching the black basses. In all waters inhabited by them, the yellow perch is a beautiful fish, and differs but slightly from its European brother of the same name. Given cool water and plenty of food, it grows to a fair size, and is then a brave fighter ; and if taken before it spawns, is succulent and even delicious as a table fish. One day last August (1893), Mr. Edward Newbury and myself took a hundred and twenty yellow perch out of Summit Lake, Washington County, New York, weighing just eighty-six pounds, and we only fished eight hours. These were all caught out of thirty feet of water, and some of them went one pound in weight. Of course in fishing for them it was necessary to take off the bob and use a light sinker, striking sharply because of the great depth. Our bait was worms. Perch also take a fly, the making of which will be explained in the chapter on fly-fishing for trout.

The white perch (*Morone Americana*) is another fish chiefly found in the estuaries of rivers in the brackish waters, and are justly much esteemed. They may be caught with the same tackle and in the same way as the sun-fishes and perch, and are to be highly recommended for their toothsomeness and the sport they give. They are generally most plentiful in early summer, and are said to feed on the ova of shad, as these fish are ascending the rivers.

CHAPTER V

FLY-FISHING FOR TROUT

No one will question my opinion that fly-fishing for trout is the very highest form of angling. It may be defined as fishing with an artificial or hand-made imitation of the natural flies and flying insects (and in some cases of jumping and crawling creatures, as in the case of crickets, grasshoppers, and grubs). In its practice only the neatest and finest of tackle is ordinarily used, the chief reason for this being the absence of all handling of living baits, and the necessity for skilful methods in order to give the lure a semblance of what other baits do or have possessed, but which this has not ; namely, life and movement.

In order that the fly may be cast lightly, as if it fell accidentally on the water, it is necessary in this form of fishing to use a rod possessing pliancy, strength, and lightness — that is *necessary* if you would be ranked as a true fly-fisherman. Of course you *can* fish with a bean-pole, as for suckers, if you choose, — this is a free country, — but there is no sense of fitness in doing so. You wouldn't write a letter home with a broom-handle ; and so I will assume that you desire to have tackle befitting the aristocratic fish you are pursuing, and that you are desirous of knowing how to use it. In such a case, without further preface, we will consider the rod.

Fly-rods for trout are of two orders, the single and double handled, — meaning for use by one or two hands. The former are chiefly in use, and only differ in that the latter are longer and heavier, and have handles so made that both hands can grasp the rod.

The single-handed trout-rod is ordinarily made of cane glued together in sections, and whipped at short intervals, and of solid woods, such as lancewood, bethabara, greenheart, etc. The cane rods are the best ; but they must be made of the very best material, and fitted with infinite skill and care, or they are worthless, as they break easily, or come apart when you least expect it ; and as the best materials and workmanship are costly, my boy readers must, I presume, be content with the other kind. A solid lancewood or greenheart makes up into a capital rod, and is far less costly ; and to give you an idea how both rods will last with care, I may say that I possess one of each wood which I have used eleven years, and they are of my own making. A fair lancewood fly-rod can be got for from five to ten dollars from the tackle stores ; but suppose my boy reader goes to work and makes one ! I will take one of my own made rods as a pattern, and we will make it together.

It is understood to be a difficult matter to ex-plain a mechanical process on paper ; but if the following instructions are followed, I do not see why there should be any failure. Of course the beginner, especially if unused to carpenter's tools, will find some trouble await him ; but "if you don't at first succeed, try, try, and try again," is all I can say to you to lighten your task.

Now, no matter what you want to build, never omit a plan of it to work from. Therefore let us make a plan of the fly-rod we are about to con-struct. The one before us is just ten feet two inches over all in length. Now take a sheet of tin, and draw a diagram with an awl and rule or

straight-edge, like Fig. 34; that is, with all the
lines and figures shown and of exactly same size.
The handle is to be ten inches long, so you deduct
that from the full length of the rod, leaving one
hundred and twelve inches. Now mark off the
figure into eight sections, and let the widest be
one-half inch, and the tip one-sixteenth inch. The
rod is taper, just as shown; that is to say, at every

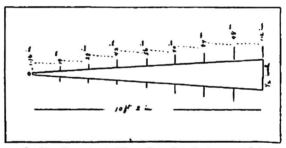

Fig. 34. — Plan cut out of Tin or Brass Plate for Lancewood Rod.

part the rod is to be just as thick through as the
diagram represents. For example, if the end of
your rod is to be half an inch in diameter, at just
half-way between it and the tip, or fifty-six inches,
it will be one-quarter inch; and the thickness the
rod should be at any point can be determined by
measurement at once. But that is not all the
advantage to be gained. Having marked the

sheet of tin or thin brass (the latter is best), just
as shown, get your hardware merchant, or do it
yourself, to cut out and file true the tapering space
between the two outer lines, leaving it exactly as
shown at Fig. 34, with the space cut out. Now
you have the plan of your rod and a gauge to
guide you in tapering it as you plane and work
the wood into shape. For example, say you are
working on the tip joint of your rod, and you want
to know how thick it should be seven inches from
the extreme tip. You just place it in the slit, and
if it fits closely half-way between 0 and 14°, it is
right ; for the diagram is divided into eight sections of fourteen inches, and seven inches are half
of each section.

(Before reading farther, go over the above again,
until you fully understand the whole thing. It is
perfectly simple, if you once grasp it, and is indispensable for you to know about.)

The tools required are neither costly nor hard
to procure. A good plane, a good wood file ; a
piece of old saw steel, some. broken glass and
sandpaper, and a jackknife and gimlet are really
all you want with which to make your first fly-rod.
I made mine with just those tools, and no more.

As you become proficient, you can extend your possessions, and get several iron planes and more files, etc.[1]

The rod is to be in three pieces, so the larger or longer joint should be of 3 ft. 8 in. (for 3 ft. 6 in.) in length, and three-fourths inch square ; the two other joints will be 3 ft. 6 in. (for 3 ft. 4 in.) each in length, and may be of half-inch and quarter-inch stuff square. Pick out some well-seasoned and straight-grained wood, and you can then go to work as follows : —

Into your work-bench drive a short hard-wood bolt, and bore holes to correspond in the ends of each of your rod pieces. This is to enable you to plane them *from* you ; and you will find this the best way always. Now commence to plane the pieces taper, keeping them square until they just fit the gauge at the proper places on it ; for example, the but-end of the large piece must be just small enough to go in the end of the plane, or measure one-half inch, and its other end must go in at the third 14-inch section ; then the but of the next just fits the third 14-inch section and the

---

[1] You can procure your wood from A. B. Shepley & Sons, 503 Commerce Street, Philadelphia ; either lancewood or greenheart.

sixth 14-inch section, and the tip or top joint at its largest part fits this sixth 14-inch section, and the tip fits the end, or is one-sixteenth of an inch in diameter.

Having got it to fit in the square, you must now take two pieces of square-edged hard wood of four-foot length each, and take a strip off one square edge of each, and then nail them together, as shown in the diagram (Fig. 35). Now lay your

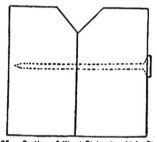

Fig. 35.—Section of Wood Strips to aid in Planing.

strip in this groove, and plane the four edges down so that each joint forms an octagon, or eight-sided stick of wood, and be particular that it is according to the gauge. Next comes the file. Now, the file must be what is known as a mill-file, and you must always use it at right angles to your work; that is, crosswise. With this rub off the eight corners of the octagon, and you will see you

are quickly progressing towards a round form for
the rod joint. At this point, the utility of the
piece of old saw comes in. Get a round file, and
file it to the shapes shown (Fig. 36), leaving three
sides plain for ordinary scraping; and you will find
this tool, when good and sharp, is a great help.
If, however, you cannot get or make this simple
tool, you must depend upon your pieces of broken
glass and file and sandpaper; and, by dint of frequent measuring and much persevering rubbing,

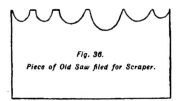

Fig. 36.
Piece of Old Saw filed for Scraper.

you will finally get it round, and of the right
diameter for each joint.

The handle of the rod must be larger, of course,
than the end of the largest joint, so that it fits the
hand comfortably. It may be made of sumach, or
some soft wood, as you please; and if you cannot
get it turned round for you by some carpenter of
your acquaintance, you must get it bored about
three inches down whilst square, and work it down

to about three-fourths inch diameter in the round, as you did the rod. At the end of it, it must be narrowed to receive the reel-fitting (Fig. 37), and the place for the hand must be swelled, as

Fig. 37. — Reel Seat.

shown (Fig. 38). You can drive the large end of your rod into it at once, cementing it with Le-Page's liquid glue.

Fig. 38. — Handle of Rod with Reel Seat in Place.

The ferrules (Fig. 39) next demand your attention. Obtain from Shipley's a set to fit the joints of your rod, and fix them on in this way. Having

Fig. 39. — Ferrule — "Male" and "Female."

got the wood so that it will go easily into the ferrules, wind it with some sewing-silk in wide coils, and saturate with the glue. Now place the ferrule on the end, and push it home. Do not put a pin into the ferrule to keep it on the rod ; that would weaken the latter.   If the ferrules work too tight, a little rotten stone and oil rubbed over them will render them freer.

The guides are now the next consideration.

Now, the guides of a fly-rod are usually of the kind shown at Fig. 40, and are whipped in place, usually during the process of winding the rod. This process consists in winding coils of silk varying from one-quarter inch to one thirty-second

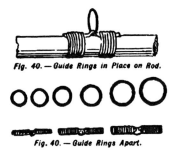

Fig. 40. — Guide Rings in Place on Rod.

Fig. 40. — Guide Rings Apart.

inch in breadth, at intervals up the rod, to strengthen it and increase its resiliency.

These whippings are made with spool-silk, to be obtained from any of the dry-goods stores ; and it should be waxed with the wax given in the chapter on sucker fishing.   There is a proper way to wind a rod, and it is as follows : Having waxed the silk, take the joint in the left hand, with the

end towards you under the left hand ; lay the silk
on the rod (Fig. 41), and turn the latter till the
end is caught under the first coil of silk, guiding
the latter with the right finger and thumb ; keep

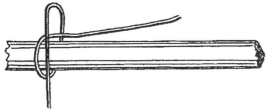

Fig. 41.— Method of commencing to wind a Rod.

turning with the left hand from you, steadying
the other end of the joint against something, — a
post will do, — and so continue till you have a
quarter of an inch (if it be the large end of the

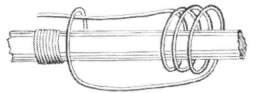

Fig. 42. — Method of finishing off winding with "Invisible" Knot.

rod) wound.   Now make the invisible knot (Fig.
42), and draw it tight by tightening the coils, and,
pulling the end through, cut off close, and it is

done. The guides need putting on in a like manner; and with a little practice this may be done as neatly as in the rods made by professionals.

The number of whippings may be varied to suit your fancy; but the more the better for the durability of your rod. There should be at least two guides on the lowest or largest joint, three on the next, and four on the tip.

Practically the rod is now ready for varnishing, and only the best coachmaker's varnish should be used. It is best to give it two or three coats with a camel's-hair brush, and to put it on thin (thinning with turpentine), taking care that each one dries before another is put on. Of course the smoother and more finished every process is, the nicer will be the appearance of the rod; and you had better get the loan of a good shop-made rod, which will remind you of each feature as you make it.

In rod-making (as in every other art) practice makes perfect, and if you do not satisfy yourself at first, *keep trying;* that is my earnest advice.

The reel for fly-fishing cannot be made at home; you must save up and buy one. The Star reels are the best and cheapest, and such a one as shown in Fig 43, called the " Gogebic," costs only a small amount, and will answer every purpose. All the tackle stores keep these reels, as they are standard.

The very finest reel in the world for fly-fishing is the Automatic, shown in Fig. 44 (p. 92). This

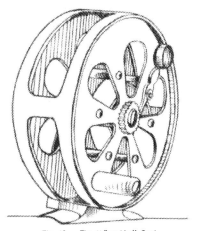

Fig. 43. — The "Gogebic" Reel.

reel winds up the line when you have hooked a fish by means of a spring released by the touch of the little finger (Fig. 45, p. 92), so that with the other hand you may use the landing-net. I, personally, never use any other.

The line for fly-fishing may be one of Martin's

Fig. 44. — " Automatic " Reel.

Fig. 45. — Showing Method of operating Spring Catch.

" Kingfisher " lines of medium thickness. If you
prefer to buy it undressed, and to dress it yourself,
do so. The following are some useful receipts : —

1. Boiled oil and best coach varnish, equal
parts ; mix at blood heat (about 100°), and immerse line twelve hours.

2. Boiled oil, one pint ; beeswax, four ounces ;
put the oil in an earthenware jar, and stand it in
boiling water. (Keep the latter boiling.) Add the
wax in small shavings. Immerse the line when
the temperature has fallen to 100°, or thereabouts,
and keep it immersed several hours, the longer the
better. The mixture should be retained at about
blood heat on the stove as long as the line is in it.

3. Boiled oil, one-half pint ; three-quarters
ounce beeswax ; one and one-half ounce Bur-
gundy pitch ; tablespoonful copal varnish. Raise
the heat of this a little above that necessary for
complete solution, and immerse the line, keeping
the mixture warm on the stove for twelve hours.

These are first-class dressings, and are decidedly
the best I know of for the boy angler. Do not
forget to wind your line on the winder (Fig. 10)
you made for your linen sucker-line, and stretch it
when soaked the proper time in some dry place

between loops of string rather than on nails. A barn makes a good place ; but, as it is apt to be dusty, an unused attic is better. Wipe off the superfluous dressing at the time of stretching with a part of an old kid glove. When it is perfectly hard and dry, a little French chalk will give it a splendid polish, if appced between the folds of a piece of chamois leather.

The next operation for the fly-fisher to learn is to make his own leaders. Now, to begin at the beginning, a leader is a line made of silkworm gut, generally three yards long ; and it is attached to the silk or reel line, and *to it* is attached the *snell* on which the fly is tied. As the silkworm gut comes in lengths, according to price, from eight inches to twenty inches in length, they must of course be joined together until the three yards is made up. Sometimes, as for bass fishing, six feet is deemed sufficient, but I prefer my leader to be within a foot of the length of the rod for trout fishing ; so nine feet let it be at this time.

The gut is cheapest if a good fair price is given for it. You can trust yourself with Shipley to send you a hank of good quality — for it comes in hanks of a hundred fibres each — at a reasonable price. There are two waste ends that are wrapped in red cotton yarn, and these must be cut off. Then immerse the strands in lukewarm soft water, and let it stand till cold. If the gut be allowed to soak all night, so much the better. In the morning proceed to make your leader, selecting only the round and even strands. You can easily see if they are round by twisting them, each end in a different direction, between finger and thumb. If flat, the gut will resemble a screw in appearance, because of the twisted flat edges. If round, no

Fig. 46. — Loop for End of Snell or Leader.

such appearance will show itself. It is well to pick out the round and clear strands, and place them in another receptacle. There are sure to be a few flat strands that can be laid aside to come in at some time when a short piece of indifferent gut will serve some odd purpose.

Assuming that you are ready to begin, — take the first strand and tie a loop (Fig. 46). This is the easiest of all the loops, though I am not quite sure that it is the best absolutely. However, I have never known it to draw loose in a long experience, and it is very easy to tie.   Draw it tight, and cut off the ends close.   The next knot to be tied is called the fisherman's knot, and is easily made (Fig. 47), and one of the best for medium thick gut ; but for the very finest the angler's knot (Fig. 48) is both easy and effective.   Either

Fig. 47. — " Fisherman's " Knot, for Leader tying.

of these will do for the tyro, as they are quickly made, strong and easy.   Other knots have been advocated even by myself, and I must refer you for these to my other books for advanced anglers.

Fig. 48. — " Angler's " Knot for Fine Gut.

Having tied up sufficient lengths to amount to nine feet, finish with another large loop.   Both of the loops should be at least one inch in length. You can now stretch the leader between two brass or clean iron nails on a board or on the side of the barn ; and when dry, being straight, it will coil neater for packing in your tackle-book.   Some

good anglers like their gut for snells and leaders
stained a mist color (a bluish dun), and this you can
do before stretching with the following stain : —

In a teacupful of hot water — nearly boiling —
drop a piece of copperas (sulphate iron), and set
that aside. Now take a piece of extract of logwood about the size of a bean, and dissolve it in
another teacupful of hot water ; add to this a good
pinch of carbonate of soda (saleratus), placing the
gut into a bowl sufficient to hold the two cups of
solution, and pouring the dissolved logwood over it.
Let it soak for fifteen minutes, till the gut has
attained a faint but decided crimson color. Then
add the copperas solution all at once (not pouring
slowly), and keep the gut moving for fifteen minutes longer. Then take out and wash with cold
water. The result is a neutral dark tint, which
renders the gut invisible on dull days, but is not,
I think, the best for bright, clear, sunny days.

The gut is best dyed *after* tying, as the stain
seems to render it less easy and smooth to tie ;
but the point is trivial and need not be insisted on.

The length of the snell is commonly four and a
half inches in American fly-making ; but Englishmen tie their flies on the whole strand, which is

sometimes, as I have said, over a foot long. The arbitrary length is on account of the fly-hook being just so long; and though not to be recommended, because the fish are liable to see the double loop of the snell and leader when it is not over four and a half inches away, the tyro can follow it for the present on account of its being convenient for the fly-hooks in general use.

Sometimes the snell is "re-enforced" by doubling the gut at the hook end. This is done by tying a large loop, and, after stretching, cutting through it (Fig. 49). Another good way is to have three strands for re-enforcement (Fig. 50); and whereas I have found two inefficient at times, I have never found three to fail with the biggest fish. The re-enforcement is also a preventive of the accident known as "cracking" off the fly, due to a clumsy cast, as will be shown farther on.

We now arrive at the daintiest art of all arts whatsoever, — fly-making. I must beg your close attention, and will at the outset promise you to give the easiest and plainest of tasks for you to do.

First, let us make the easiest of all artificial flies together, a " Pennell Hackle." Take a snell of gut, and a feather (hackle) from the neck of a

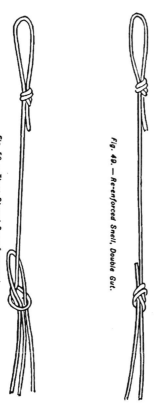

Fig. 50. — Three Strand Re-enforcement.

Fig. 49. — Re-enforced Snell, Double Gut.

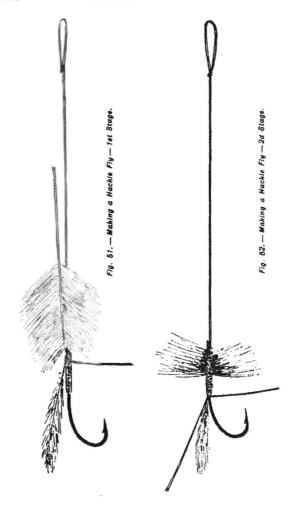

Fig. 51. — Making a Hackle Fly — 1st Stage.

Fig. 52. — Making a Hackle Fly — 2d Stage.

rooster ; also a hook and a waxed piece of spool-
silk.   Place the snell underneath
the shank of the hook, and whip
it with the silk and the end of
the hackle (Fig. 51), taking care
the hackle is placed with the
under side *up*.   Then take the
quill end of the hackle, and
wind it round at right angles to
the shank (Fig. 52), and finally
tie it in place, and run the silk
down to opposite the barb of
the hook, leaving the end of the
hackle protruding to form the
tail of the fly.   When finished,
it appears as shown in Fig. 53.
This fly may be made without
other tools than the fingers ; but
for all other kinds, some other
tools are advisable.   These are
as follows : —

A vice made somewhat after
the diagram (Fig. 54).

A pair of pliers made of steel
wire (Fig. 55).

Fig. 53.—*Making a Hackle*
Fly — 3d Stage.

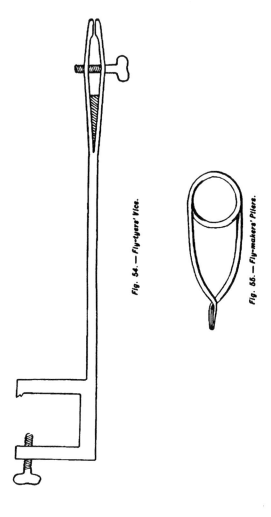

Fig. 54. — Fly-tyers' Vice.

Fig. 55. — Fly-makers' Pliers.

A little hook made from a crochet hook, to draw the thread through in tying knots ; and on the other end you can roll your wax, as the stick enables you to rub it on the silk with less risk of getting it on your fingers.

The wax needed is as formulated in the chapter on sucker fishing.

The varnish is of white (or bleached) shellac.

The feathers you need will depend upon the kind of fly made, of course, and consist of hundreds of varieties, though you can make killing flies with few. Never disdain the wings of any bird, or the hackles of any rooster. They are always useful.

The silks used for the bodies of flies are the best "wash" embroideries. The tinsel is the flat kind, to be purchased at the theatrical costume-makers ; but if you find a difficulty in this material, send to Shipley's, or substitute yellow or white silk for the gold or silver tinsel. In most cases this can be done without hurting the usefulness of the fly.

For the beginner I advise the following modest list of feathers : —

Hackles, from brown, black, Plymouth Rock, and white roosters.

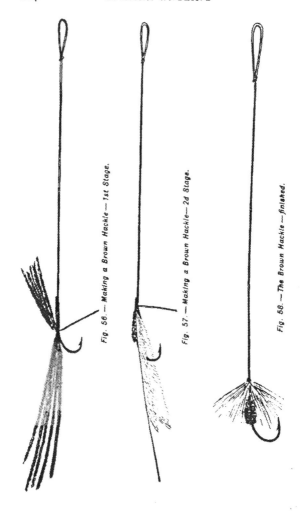

Fig. 56. — Making a Brown Hackle — 1st Stage.

Fig. 57. — Making a Brown Hackle — 2d Stage.

Fig. 58. — The Brown Hackle — finished.

Wings from the crow, white goose, brown hen, and mallard duck, with feathers from the breast of the latter, turkey tail feathers, peacock tail or sword feathers.

The silks to be used can be procured as they are wanted from any dry-goods store.

Let us now make a hackle fly, say a brown hackle, which is a killing fly everywhere for trout, and will probably take more fish in a year than any other one fly known to anglers in five years. Set your vice in place on the edge of a good firm table. Take a No. 6 Sproat hook (see Fig. 33), and tie a snell to it, commencing an eighth part of the shank away from the end (for there is where your head of the fly will be, and you don't want it to be too large). Now take two of three fibres of the peacock's tail feathers (called herl), and tie in the ends as shown (Fig. 56); wind them round the shank till within one-eighth of an inch of the end; and now wind your tying silk around the herl, that is, wound in a loose coil to where you want the herl to be secured (one-eighth of an inch from the end). Now tie the herl with a half-hitch (Fig. 57), and cut off the loose part.

Now take a hackle, and, by stroking it from

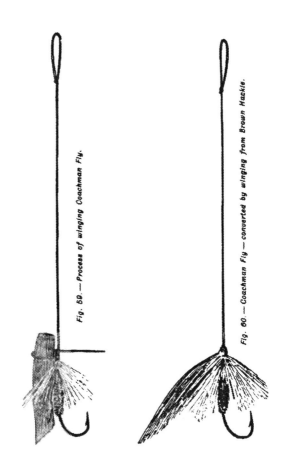

Fig. 59.—Process of winging Coachman Fly.

Fig. 60. — Coachman Fly — converted by winging from Brown Hackle.

end to end, draw out the fibres. Run the nail of the middle finger of the right hand down next the mid-rib, holding the *point* of the hackle between the finger and thumb of the right hand, and the root of it between the forefinger and thumb of the left hand. The nail of the middle finger can be forced in this way against the roots of the fibres, and they will be "*turned*," as it is termed (Fig. 57), and so arranged away from the mid-rib that they will not be tangled up when tied on the hook. This little operation should be mastered, as it is of great value to the fly-maker.

Now cut off the extreme tip of the hackle, and tie it in (Fig. 57); then wind it as you did with the Pennell hackle, and tie it firmly with the tying silk, with two half-hitches; cut off the loose ends of the silk and hackle, touch with the varnish, and your Brown Hackle is finished.

Now, in the making of a winged fly, let us take the "Coachman," which is a Brown Hackle with a white wing added. The easiest way is to so dress the Brown Hackle as to leave space enough when the hackle is tied to lay on a pair of wings taken from two feathers (Fig. 59) — from opposite wing feathers of the white goose or pigeon. The slips of feather are held between the forefinger and thumb of the left hand, and pressed down to the shank of the hook; then the thread is passed up and over the ends of the slips, and down round the shank, and there secured (Figs. 59 and 60). These are called *laid* on wings; and small white whole feathers will do equally as well as slips, and may be tied with less difficulty. Indeed, in the large-sized bass fly a pair of feathers is always used.

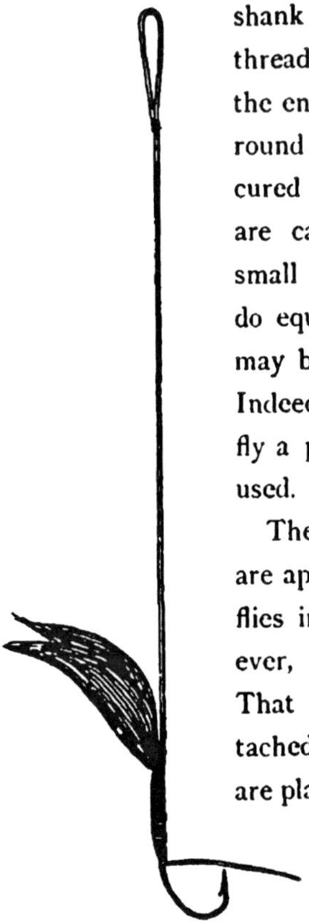

The " reversed " wings, which are applied to all the best trout flies in this country, are, however, put on the hook *first*. That is, when the hook is attached to the snell, two slips are placed in the position shown (Fig. 61), and there secured. Then the body and legs, or hackle, are tied as in the case of

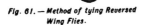

Fig. 61. — *Method of tying Reversed Wing Flies.*

the Brown Hackle fly; and after the hackle is secured, the wings are turned back and secured with two half-hitches, and the fly is finished.

The learner has only to practise making these two flies till he can find no fault with them, to understand the whole principle of fly-making. And he can catch fish with one or the other of these all days in the trout season. Of course, as he gets other patterns to imitate, he will want to search the works on angling for the names of the materials used, and it will be necessary for him to sometimes undo a fly (from the head) to find out how it is made; but with perseverance he will soon learn the process, and will only thus be doing what many others have done before. Mr. Francis Francis, the great English angling author and editor of the *Field*, admitted that he had never had a lesson on fly-making in his life, yet he was certainly an excellent fly-maker, to my certain knowledge.

As I have mentioned a few materials that the tyro had better provide himself with, I will give the flies they are useful for : —

Brown Hackle, — peacock herl body, brown hackle for legs.

Black Hackle, — black embroidery silk body, black hackle for legs.

Plymouth Rock Hackle, — green silk body, ribbed with gold tinsel or yellow silk, and the hackle 'for legs.

White Hackle, — white silk body, ribbed silver tinsel, hackle at head for legs.

Black June is made thus : *Body*, peacock herl ; *legs*, black hackle ; *wings*, crow.

Coachman has been described.

Cowdun, — body, yellowish green wool yarn ; legs, brown hackle ; wings, from the brown hen.

Red Spinner, — body, blood-red silk ; legs, brown hackle ; wings, from the leaden part of the wing feathers of the mallard duck.

Professor, — body, yellow silk ribbed with gold tinsel, and a tuft of red ibis feathers (you can get ibis sufficient for this from me) as tail ; legs, brown hackle ; wings, two breast feathers of the mallard.

Montreal, — body, wine-colored silk, ribbed gold tinsel ; legs, a wine-colored hackle (stained or dyed, from the white rooster hackles) ; wings, turkey tail feather.

These flies will be sufficient for the young fly-maker to begin on ; and when he has mastered them, he must go for further information to my

more advanced book, " Fly-fishing and Fly-making," published by the " Forest & Stream Co.,"
New York City ; or he can send to mè direct,
and I will advise and help him, so that he cannot
fail.

I spoke of *stained* hackles just now.   The
staining can be done very easily by means of the
" Diamond Dyes," to be got at any drug-store.
Be sure you follow the " directions " exactly —
they are given on each ten-cent package of dye.
The feathers must be washed with soap and warm
water until every particle of the natural grease is
out, and rinsed in several waters, to get out the
soap.   They are best dried, after dying and rinsing
in cold water, by placing them in a cardboard box,
pierced with holes through the lid, and letting
them get warm on the stove ; or, if the weather be
favorable, out in the air, shaking the box vigor-
ously every now and again.   This is my practice
for a large quantity.   For a small number (a few
dozen or so), tie the hackles on ordinary skewers,
or slips of wood, a dozen on each ; and when you
want to dry them you can do so by simply twirl-
ing them between the palms of both hands.

Having constructed your fly, I must now tell

you how to use it, — and let me here say that the most successful fly-fisher is he who knows how to drop his fly daintily, rather than he who only knows how to cast a long line. Most fish are caught within fifty feet ; and you need not, therefore, endeavor to learn how to cast ninety feet at the first start.

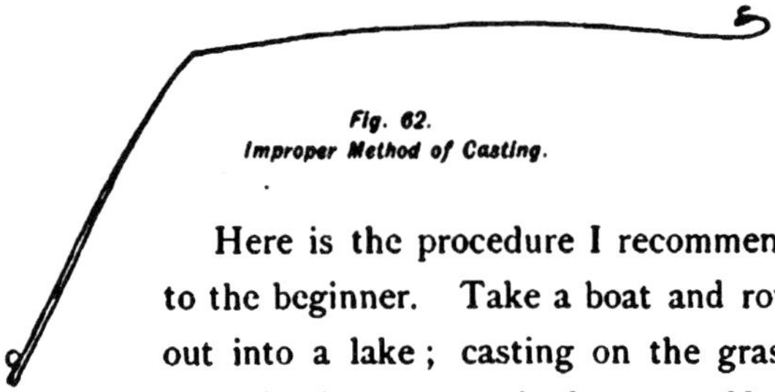

Fig. 62.
Improper Method of Casting.

Here is the procedure I recommend to the beginner. Take a boat and row out into a lake ; casting on the grass *will* do, but water is better. Now grasp your fly-rod firmly by the handle ; the reel *below* the hand (no matter what anybody else says), and hanging from the rod ; the grasp should be as shown in Fig. 45 ; and if you use the automatic reel, the little finger must go round the break, as shown, but not on it, except where necessary to draw out line or land a fish. Draw out from the reel a few yards of line, and, waving the rod with a smart movement, cause it to pass through the guides. The cast is made by drawing

the rod smartly backwards, so as to throw the fly
back in the air to the extent of the line out ; and
then a forward thrash of the rod brings the fly
forward, and lays the line out straight. It is a
matter of judgment, based on much practice, to
know when to bring the rod again forward ; but
practice and watching others are the only roads

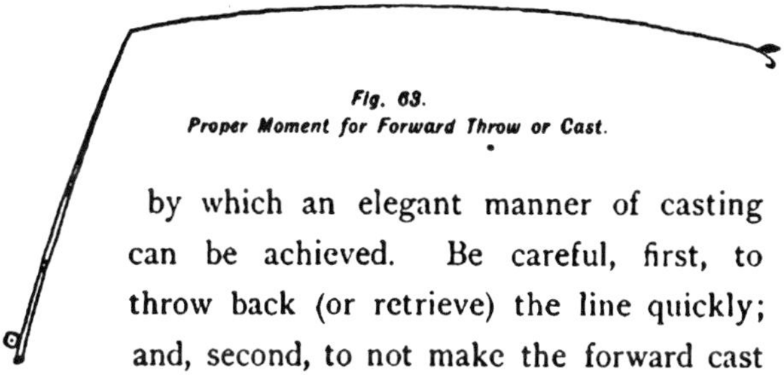

Fig. 63.
Proper Moment for Forward Throw or Cast.

by which an elegant manner of casting
can be achieved. Be careful, first, to
throw back (or retrieve) the line quickly;
and, second, to not make the forward cast
or throw too quickly thereafter. If you do, the
result is shown in Fig. 62, where the fly has not
got back far enough, and the forward movement
snaps the fly off (most probably on the principle
of the snap of a whip). Fig. 62 shows the *improper* forward cast, and Fig. 63 the *proper* moment at which the cast should be made.

Again I say, practice, practice, practice ! If you
do so on the grass, tie a little tuft of wool yarn
on your line end ; and I have found the snow in

winter to be a capital fly-casting ground. As
soon as you, can lay out thirty feet straight and
without snapping, go to work and strive for deli-
cacy and correctness of aim, especially the former.
It is unpardonable to make a splash of your line
in the water when fly-fishing.

We now come to an important point, — *how to
fly-fish.* On this subject volumes have been written ; and, as Izaak Walton long ago pointed out,
one might as well try to teach another how to use
his fists in writing as to try to teach fishing in
the same way ; nevertheless, if the learner will let
this little book accompany his persistent practice,
he will be on the right road towards becoming a
proficient fly-caster and trout fisherman.

If the stream to be fished is a tolerably broad
and slow-flowing one, the dry fly may be used ;
and this means that the fly is dried in the air by
several times making the motion of casting, but
not dropping the fly. In England, especially on
the clear chalk streams, this fishing is the only
style deemed ordinarily applicable ; but it is rarely
used in this country, though I frequently practise
it, having had at one time ten miles of the premier
dry-fly stream of England in my charge. And

the fly in this style must be cast *up* stream, not *down*, and be allowed to float until it approaches the feet of the angler. This is a deadly style of fishing ; but the flies must be small, and require to be made with large wings, and sometimes it is advisable to use double wings ; that is, *two* slips for each wing instead of one.

The ordinary way of fly-fishing is, however, to cast the fly down stream and across, drawing it up with slightly jerking motion. This motion expands and contracts the fibres of the fly, and gives a semblance of life, as if the insect struggled to be free ; and this movement, of course, goes far to hide the fraud on the fish. In dry-fly fishing this movement is not made, but the fly is allowed to float quite without movement ; and is necessarily, therefore, of much closer imitation, — that is, to be successful. Personally, I am an advocate of the "exact imitation" theory, and believe that all imitations should be as close as possible. This is, however, a refinement into which the boy-angler need not be led.

Down-stream fishing is certainly easier to practise, and the task of casting is much facilitated by the downward and therefore *pulling* action of the water

Of course all likely spots must be covered, whether they lie down or up stream, — quiet corners and eddies ; the edges and, in early summer, the centre of swift-running streams ; beneath dams ; near old sunken trunks of trees or logs ; near to springs and cool incoming streams ; and though no special time of the day can absolutely be set apart, yet early morning and late afternoon are generally found most fruitful of sport in trout fishing.

Nor is the night-time to be despised in midsummer. During the excessive heat of the day no fish will bite ; but if the moon be on the ascendant, or even on the decline, providing it be not *too* bright, trout will rise to the fly very satisfactorily in the night. Indeed, the fact that no fish are so easily taken in the daytime whilst there are moonlight nights, may be assumed to be because the fish find food plenteously at night-time, and therefore have no room for it in the daytime ; or, at least, do not feel so eager as they otherwise would do. For night fishing large flies are best ; a large Brown Hackle or Coachman is a capital lure, and it can be cast into the water with some splashing, for the purpose of attracting the fish's attention. Some of the largest fish are taken in this way ; though, to be sure, it is rather lonesome work, unless one is accompanied by another brother of the rod.

Another very productive way of fly-fishing is angling with what is known in England as a " blow-line." This consists of a light floss or twist silk reel line, and a single hook at the end of the leader, on which is impaled a natural fly — a " blow " or blue-bottle fly is the best. The only time this lure can be used is when the wind is favorable. It must be at your back, blowing either up, or up and across, or down, or down and across ; but, as you can fish from either bank, you have a good choice of winds, and can fish quite a number of days in the summer. It is especially fitted for fishing the riffles or shallows, and is very killing.

The way to practise it is as follows : First, catch your blue-bottles — the butcher will gladly spare you what he has, and a gauze insect collector's net is the most useful device for their capture. Then kill them by pinching their heads ; next tie a fine piece of silk thread around each one ; prepare, say, two dozen in this way before repairing to the stream. You will not regret the time it

Being on the bank of the river, you must find out about the wind ; for to it you owe the placing of your fly where the fish are. Having slipped the hook into the girdle of silk thread round the fly, you raise your rod aloft, and begin drawing out your fine silk line. The looser the strands of the line the better, as the wind catches it the more readily when it is loosely twisted. Let it float out before the wind, till some forty feet or more are being blown up or down over the stream. Then by lowering the point of the rod, drop your fly just on the water, let it float a few inches, and lift the rod again, so as to take it off, continuing to do this over any likely spots you may perceive. It is rare that a trout refuses to rise to this lure, and there is really more in it than seems to be the case from this brief mention.

Fly-fishing with the natural fly is to be commended as a killing method of fishing at all times where possible ; but it does not compare with fishing with the artificial fly as an art.

A word of advice may here fitly be given in reference to the playing and landing of a hooked trout. Don't forget that you must never allow the fish a slack line ; keep the tip of the rod always

up and at tension against the fish ; be careful and
deliberate ; never hurry the fish ; and, finally, never
lift the fish by the line, — use a landing-net, and
bring it up behind the fish, rather than dive for
the head of the fish, as I have seen novices do
many times. If the fish is not tired out, let it
struggle until it is, and *then* you can use the net,
if you cannot do so at first.

CHAPTER VI

FLY-FISHING FOR BASS, PERCH, SUNFISH, ETC.

IN summer, especially during the early part of July, the bass (both " large " and " small " mouth) will take the fly with avidity. A rather more powerful rod is necessary to completely enjoy bass fly-fishing ; but the one made for trout will do if a tip be fashioned rather shorter — say six inches — than the one you use for trout. The reason for this requirement is the heavier and larger fly in use. It is usually twice as large as the ordinary ones employed for trout ; and for the large-mouth bass of the South, I have made flies nearly three inches long, but these are very exceptional. A No. 3 or 4 hook (see Fig. 33) is ordinarily large enough for the black basses of the generality of our streams and lakes.

The reel need not be changed, and that employed for trout can be used without difficulty. The line may be a little thicker, but the point is of no importance if it be strong enough. I always use my trout fly-line for black bass, and find no difficulty. The leader should be of thicker gut, and the same length as for trout.

If you have carefully followed the directions for fly-making for trout, you do not need them repeated here; for bass fly-making is identical in principle and practice, except that a larger hook and stouter gut are used. A few of the best bass flies I know of may be described, and with these you will probably catch as many fish as anybody else with a $500 collection. These have the merit, also, of simplicity : —

Brown Hackle, — made as described for trout on No. 3 or 4 hook.

Brown Moth, — body, brown worsted (cinnamon brown) ; tail, a few hairs from tail of brown squirrel ; legs, brown hackle ; wings, turkey tail. Size of hook, No. 3.

Coachman (see chapter on trout).

Royal Coachman, — made same as ordinary Coachman, but the body is divided in centre by a band of scarlet silk. (Fig. 64.)

Gray Hackle, — same as for trout. No. 3 hook.

Professor, — same as for trout. No. 3 hook.

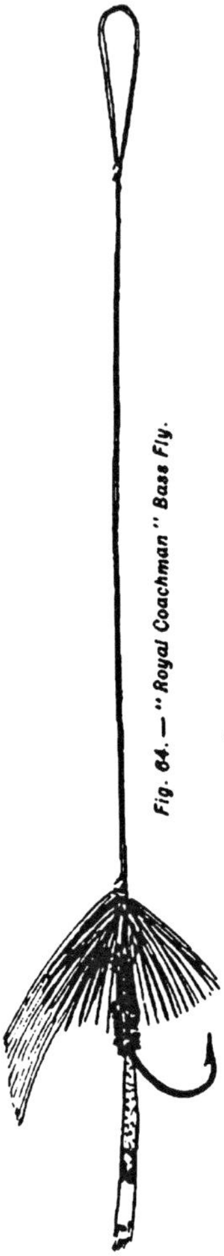

Fig. 64. — " Royal Coachman " Bass Fly.

Black June, — same as for trout. No. 3 hook.

Cowdun, — brown wings ; greenish-yellow worsted body ; brown hackle.

White Miller, — body, white wool and silk-ribbed gold tinsel, or orange silk ; hackle, white ; wings, white.

Seth Green, — body, green silk ribbed with yellow silk ; wings, brown (buff turkey tail) ; hackle, brown. No. 3 hook. These are sufficient to begin with.

In using the fly for bass, somewhat similar tactics to those in vogue for trout are employed. Of course the thing to do first is to ascertain beyond peradventure that bass are present. The fly is cast in precisely the same style as for trout ; but it is allowed to sink several inches at least under water before it is drawn back by little jerks towards the caster. In deep water it is advisable to close a small split shot about a foot above the hook, so that the line is sunk a foot, or even two, beneath the water. The small-mouth black bass is usually found over a rocky bottom, near old submerged trunks of trees, and in deeper water generally than its *confrère* of the "large-mouth" species. But both take the fly greedily at times; and when either is hooked, there is quite a "circus" on hand to deal with. Especially is this so with the small-mouth fish. He is the very bull-dog of the water. As soon as the hook pricks him, the line runs out with startling rapidity; then he leaps from the water, following this up with other leaps, sometimes to the number of six, or even more; and it is necessary to be patient and wary if you would secure the fish in the end. I do not think any fish that swims is superior to the black basses in fighting-power on the hook.

By the way, the young angler is sometimes puzzled to know how to distinguish between the *large*-mouth and the *small*-mouth fish. Let him do it by observing the feature that gives them their colloquial names. The large-mouth has a proportionately much larger mouth, extending to the outer orbit or rim enclosing the eye, whilst in the small-mouth, the mouth only extends to a line drawn perpendicularly through the centre of the pupil of the eye, and in addition there is a spot of red in the eye of the latter.

All the various black basses of fresh water in this country have been decided by authoritative naturalists to belong to one of these species: either *Micropterus salmoides* (the large-mouth), or *M. dolimeu* (the small-mouth black bass).

I have at times dressed the flies I used with a slip of lead on the hook shank under the body; but it has the disadvantage of interfering with the casting. The fly does not alight so softly, and cannot be propelled through the air so readily. The movement in bass-fly casting should be almost exactly like that in throwing a ball; and I suppose my boy readers know how this is done overhand.

Perch will take the fly in summer in any waters where they are numerous. Near where I write is a beautiful little mountain lake on the summit of a hill (whence it is termed Summit Lake), supplied by springs, and deep and clear and cool. Bass and perch inhabit it; and the perch vie with the bass in taking the fly. Whilst camping on its

shores last August, I found that a special fly was
wanted to withstand the sharp teeth of the perch ;
and after many experiments I found the following to be the most killing combination. It is a
modification of the ever useful "Coachman." I
call it the Bronze Coachman : —

Body, of the bronze tinsel cord one gets at the
dry-goods stores at five cents or so a ball. It is
used by ladies for embroidering on velvet, etc.
Legs, plenty of brown hackle ; wings, white.

With this fly we sometimes caught three perch
on a line at one time ; of course using three
flies. These flies were made on a No. 6 hook.
(See Fig. 33.)

A Brown Hackle is a capital fly also for perch.
So is what is known as the Soldier Palmer. This
fly has a red silk or woollen yarn body ; and one
hackle is tied in at the bend of the hook or tail
end of the body, and run up in several coils to
the head, and there fastened ; another one is then
tied in at the head in the ordinary way.

Either of these flies will also catch the lively
little sun-fishes ; and I do not by any means disdain this small fry, if fished for on the trout-rod
with fine gut and small hooks.

The wall-eyed pike, white perch, and even pickerel, will take a fly ; and in the waters of Florida
almost every fish that swims will respond to a
gaudy fly or insect.   I therefore strongly advise
my boy readers to make the fly-rod and its acces-
sories their chief thought in fishing.   Fly-fishing
is the fine art of angling, and they will never regret the time and pains expended on it.   The lord
of all sporting fishes is the salmon, and he is
chiefly captured with the beautiful creations of
the fly-makers' fingers.   In the years of maturity
my readers will doubtless come to fish for and
catch this superb fish, and these pages are intended as preparatory lessons for so doing.   But
all *must* begin with this alphabet before going
farther.

The memories of many adventures in pursuit of
fish with the fly-rod arise in my mind as I approach the end of this chapter, and I am minded
to tell of a coincidence that occurs to me now
when thoughts of summer fly-fishing are com-
manding the attention.

A fish-story, to be generally palatable, must be
very highly spiced with romance.   This one is a
record of veritable experience.

My narrative really consists of two separate stories, each being perfectly distinct and complete in itself. The incidents occurred many years and thousands of miles apart. But coincidence connects them with each other in the fact that they both occurred on the same date, May 1st, and that their salient features were alike, as were also their results. " So much," to quote old Izaak Walton, " for the prologue of what I mean to say."

I was born on the banks of the English Thames ; how long ago it does not boot to say. My father, and generations of his ancestors, were professional Thames fishermen, so it is easy to understand that I loved and learned fishing as soon as I could walk — nay, I am given to understand that I caught my first fish *before* I could walk. Be that as it may, I could handle a rod long before most boys hear of one, and I was a constant companion of my father whenever possible. He was a *great* fisherman, — I say it advisedly, — keen of eye, intuitive, an athlete, and a fish lover, and particularly was he a great trout-fisherman. The Thames trout is a brown trout (*Salmo fario*), and grows to sixteen pounds on exceptional occasions, and averages, or did, from seven to ten

pounds. He is a *rara avis* of the water, I am
bound to admit. But my progenitor rarely failed
to capture the " sockdolager " of every dam or
" weir " above the tideway each season. He had
his own methods. Here they are, in brief : The
rod was a light red deal and lancewood rod of
some fourteen feet (he was tall) ; the line was
a fine strong silk one ; the leader was a six-foot
length of good stout gut ; and the *one* hook — no
gangs of ten for him — was a No. 1 Sproat or
Limerick. His bait was a small fish named bleak
or bley, similar to, but brighter than, a " shiner."
The manner of using this outfit was simple.
These large trout frequent the deep, quiet waters
adjacent to the rough waters of the dams or
" weirs," and there in some corner watch, in perhaps twenty feet of water, for what they may dis-
cover. Now, above and some eight or ten feet
over these dams is built a beam as a bridge-way —
a single beam, without railings ; for the public
were not supposed to use it. Only danger-lov-
ing English boys would dare to run along its
dizzy path and gaze into the tumbling water below ; the general public never intruded. This
beam always formed the coign of vantage on

which my father — and none but himself hitherto, owing to the dizzying effect — had taken his stand for the glorious Thames trout. From this standpoint the bait was manipulated deftly across and athwart the rushing waters; and there was frequently ten or fifteen yards of loose line drawn from the reel and coiled in a figure eight in the hand preparatory to casting. Many a time had I watched his dexterous movements with envy; and once, after aiding to boat a particularly large fish, I remember the resolve was suddenly born in my boyish heart that I would, could, and must do likewise.

The fishing season began in April, but was best a little later; and behold me, therefore, one bright May Day morning, a boy of about twelve, early in the light skiff, eager to reach the vicinity of the "weir." I remember the joy I felt: it comes back to me now; and also the scent of the hawthorn hedges, with their masses of white bloom; the carol of the skylark, the song of the thrush and the blackbird, and even the brilliant azure and orange-red hues of the kingfisher as he darted by — all nature was radiant! I soon reached the venerable weir; and, selecting with a general's eye the most "likely" spot, I made the boat fast, and

climbed lightly on to the beam. Very soon I was
sitting astride it, and deftly casting the brilliant
minnow, and manœuvring it from cataract to eddy
through the myriad jewelled spray. As it skipped
and danced from crest to crest, it seemed like some
silvern butterfly rather than a fish. Herein lay its
attraction ; and before I had fished twenty minutes
the great tortoise-shell shoulders of a big trout
heaved above the torrent, and with a determined
plunge he had seized the bait, and sunk for his
watery lair. How well I remember the thrill of
awe-like ecstasy I felt ! And then began the battle. I will not attempt its description. Such com-
bats have been portrayed by more masterly pens
than mine. It is sufficient to say that, from my
high post, it was one of tragic interest to me as
well as the fish ; and just as the latter seemed to
become sufficiently amenable to reason to allow of
my seeking the shore, with a view to landing him,
I remember the top of my head seemed to be
swimming off somewhere ; then the water became
sheets of silver flame — I staggered, recovered myself, for I had risen on the narrow bridge, the better to traverse it shoreward ; then the loose line
dropped from my left hand, and, without further

to-do, I rolled off into the boiling torrent below, — down — down — down to the abysmal depths. The cold water revived my mind, and with a good diver's prescience I held my breath, and sought to emerge from the curling, eddying, twisting fury of the maelstrom of which I was the sport. Try as I would, I found my arms and legs held as in a vice, and powerless; then after a time, interminable as it seemed, I was violently thrust forward, as by some strong human arm, and found I was ascending. With one convulsive kick I arose amidst a great clot of white foam, which I remember to this day looked like a great sky window from below. My breath came back convulsively, and, oh how painfully and chokingly! and in another moment I was washed on to the shallow riffle ten or twelve rods below the dam. There I lay for quite a time, till I could cough up what water I had unavoidably swallowed. Finally, I began to realize. The first poignant thought was the fish. The loose line had wound round and round my legs and body, and even arms, in the eddy; but still something was attached to it. This was the rod. Carefully I drew it up unbroken and reeled in the line, which I had disengaged from my body. There was still a lot of

line in the water, apparently entangled *up stream*.
I unsteadily wound it in — it was fast around the
woodwork of the dam.   I tried to draw it to me
— then suddenly out sped the still attached fish.
Was ever such good fortune ?   Reader, *I fought
that fish anew, and landed him.   He weighed seven
and a quarter pounds !*   He should have been lost
to me, I know, according to usage in all fishing
stories, but — I cannot tell a lie !

This occurred at Chertsey Weir, England, A.D.
1867 ; and many yet live near the spot who can
attest the occurrence.

My second episode occurred in 1891, at the East
Greenwich Dam, Batten Kill River, Washington
Co., N.Y.   Time of year, also May 1st.   A glorious morning for the fisherman was this when I
drove up to Lake's Hotel " as the gray dawn was
breaking."   The robins were still at matins around
the house, and very soon I had mine host and his
satellites roused.   A keen sportsman he ; and to his
salutation I returned, " Is the dam in good order
for fishing ? " receiving an affirmative reply in no
uncertain tone.   No boat being on the river, I had
taken my " Acme " canvas folding boat, intending
to fly-fish all the likely spots of this famous trout

water. Very soon I had the boat geared ; and whilst one of the men carried her to the water, I took my " morning draught," as quaint old Walton would term it. That duly accomplished, and with rod lightly arranged, I stepped into the fragile bark, and was pushed off into the stream.

In this instance I was below the dam, and intended approaching as near as might be advisable, and anchoring, altering positions to suit circumstances. A select crowd had gathered on the shore, and were taking in the situation with enjoyment ; and I soon increased their admiration by boating a nice little twelve-ounce fish. Now, this dam was built for supplying a knitting and flour mill near by, and is not at all a formidable one, its fall not being more than ten feet ; but at the time of which I am writing, a very respectable volume of water was coming over, and there was, at one part near the side, a swift and powerful undertow, — a fact of which I was yet unaware. Presently, however, a good fish rose to my Royal Coachman ; and as I struck him, and saw him plunge, I knew it was a two-pounder at least. How he did fight ! And finally, finding I should have trouble in boating him, the boat being so light, and I being so heavy for it, I determined to raise anchor and let her drift to the shallow water, where I could step out and accomplish the deed. The raising of the stone anchor I easily accomplished with one hand, and then prepared to manage the fish. As the boat drifted, however, I found she took a rather erratic course, which, being so light (seventy pounds only), I attributed to the pressure I was putting on the fish. At all events, I suddenly realized that we were in the undertow, and rapidly approaching the dam's fullest rush of water. Once under that, and, with my heavy boots and other paraphernalia, I was doomed. I tried to row her free, but the hold of that fell stream was great. Still I should have rescued her had not the light oar broken. Then, when there was nothing else to do, I jumped ; and, as fortune would have it, I escaped by some miraculous means the force of the reflecting current, and, with nothing more than a good ducking and some excitement, I swam as best I could, and was pulled out on *terra firma*.

What of the boat ? Well, released from my weight, she floated on the upper stratum of the current, and was stranded a few hundred yards lower down. And " what of the fish ? " do you ask. M' yes, I cannot tell a lie. I didn't find it still on. It broke loose! *But it weighed just two pounds seven ounces, all the same.* I am positive of that. And this is how I know : —

Two months later I was fishing the dam of a flax-mill lower down the same river. It was evening ; and as the soft-winged moths fluttered alongside my own artificial white miller, I "rose" a fish and hooked him. Moreover, I landed him ; and in his mouth were the remains of my identical Royal Coachman fly, lost at the upper dam in the early season. No one makes this fly just as I do. This fish weighed two pounds seven ounces exactly, — that is why I am positive of the weight of the lost one, you see !

PART III

AUTUMN ANGLING

CHAPTER VII

MINNOW-FISHING FOR TROUT

IT is not usual to fish with a minnow for any
trout except the *Salmo namaycush*, or Great Lake
trout, in this country; but those who have tried
it for brook trout, including myself, find it quite
as deadly as the fly or worm. I shall not describe
the process of trolling for the lake trout, as it is a
sport that is rather outside the reach of my young
readers, further than to say a gang of hooks, on
which a shiner is impaled, as in pickerel trolling,
is ordinarily used, or one of the artificial fish (the
" Caledonian " Minnow or " Phantom " Bait) is
attached to the line and towed behind a boat precisely as in pickerel trolling — in principle, though
the detail may vary. The Great Lake trout is
taken in spring and fall by this method, and a
grand fish it is; but if one can use the minnow
for the brook trout, he may be pretty certain that
the lake trout fisherman can teach him but little
concerning the larger fish.

Now, the minnow is only used for brook trout on rivers where it is known large trout exist. These large fellows are also very hard to catch with the fly or bait, and hence it is not unsportsmanlike to use the live or dead minnow. In no case need the young sucker, dace, or shiner be longer than two and one-half inches; and sometimes, if smaller, the sport resulting will be the more.

The live minnow must first claim our attention. Be sure they are got from some cool stream, if you are to use them near springs, where the large trout do most congregate at this season of the year. If you do not pay attention to this little matter, they will not live and play freely on the hook, any more than an African from Central Africa would find the climate of the Esquimau to his liking; but they will certainly die, and that sometimes as soon as they touch the cooler water.

The tackle you must use for the live minnow may be one single No. 2 hook on strong gut, with a light sinker to carry the bait down, or it may be like that figured; namely, a single loop hook to go through the bait's lip, and a triplet hook to lie by side the bait (Fig. 65). In the case of the single-hook tackle there is a good chance of hooking the fish, but in the case of the triplet hook arrangement the chance is far better; and especially is this tackle fitted for use in the rapid water of dams, etc., where the biggest fish undoubtedly lie. The triplet hook simply lies alongside the living minnow, and it is worked around in the likely places pretty much as any other bait, taking all the care you can, of course, not to get

Fig 65. — *Gang for Live-minnow Fishing for Trout.*

"hung up" on the stones or sunken logs, boughs, etc.

Sometimes, when trout are found to inhabit the deep springs of lakes, a large glass jar may be filled with minnows, and closed, and lowered by a line near their hovers, and allowed to remain. Perch and trout both are attracted by this lure, and I know of several instances where the method has been exceedingly successful. There are no further hints to be given on this head, except two words of advice. Keep your bait moving, and use

lively minnows.   When they die, take them off
and place away in a little piece of tissue paper, in
your can or basket, for another style of fishing;

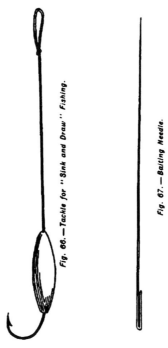

Fig. 66.—Tackle for " Sink and Draw " Fishing.

Fig. 67.—Baiting Needle.

viz., dead-minnow fishing, which is frequently more
deadly than fishing with the live bait.

The particular form of dead-bait fishing I prefer
to all others is that known as the " sink and

draw " bait. To prepare the tackle, you take a
single hook, about No. 3 (Fig. 33), and, having
tied it to double or extra thick gut, slide upon
it a barrel lead or sinker (Fig. 66) ; let this be
plugged, so that the lead stays as shown. To use
it, a bait of suitable size is selected, — it must be
dead, of course, or you will kill it ; and, if dead, it
must be fresh, — and a baiting-needle (Fig. 67),
made by turning the end of a thin piece of iron
or brass wire, is attached to the loop of the gut
by the eye. The needle is now entered into the
fish by the mouth, and brought out exactly in the
centre of the tail ; the gut is drawn through, and,
finally, the lead is pulled into the stomach of the
bait, leaving the hook to hang around its mouth
sufficiently rank or outstanding to easily hook any
fish that swallows it. The tail of the bait is tied
round with a piece of thread, to keep the gut from
tearing out if the tail catches in anything ; and the
piece of tackle is now ready to be attached to the
reel line. The latter should be fine, and not a
heavy one, and the rod needs to be light and
moderately pliant.

Having attached the bait, a few yards of line
are drawn off the reel with the left hand, and the

bait is gently *urged* through the air, rather than
cast to any suitable eddy or spot likely to hold a
trout.   Letting the point of the rod droop, the
bait " shoots headlong through the blue abyss," as

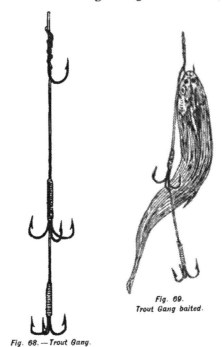

Fig. 69.
Trout Gang baited.

Fig. 68. — Trout Gang.

a poet has aptly described the motion.   That is
the " sink " of the " sink and draw " bait-fishing.
After a little pause the point of the rod is gently

lifted, and a foot or two of the line gathered in, and the bait is again allowed to shoot downward. It is generally at the moment of the headlong plunge of the bait that the trout darts out and takes the bait.   If, on drawing up, you find that vicious tug! tug! which infallibly denotes a fish, just lower the point of the rod a few seconds, and then strike sharply.   In nine cases out of ten you will hook the fish, and must proceed to land him. You will find that in every case your fish will be the largest, not the smallest, of the stream.

A gang of small hooks (Fig. 68) is easily made, and is very effective if plenty of swivels are placed above it, to prevent the line kinking when the bait revolves, as it will do when baited (Fig. 69).   I, however, recommend the other "sink and draw" tackle in preference ; though such a gang is very useful to have with one in the event of see-ing a large trout unexpectedly, which will take no other bait.   A small artificial minnow is also emi-nently useful at times, and sometimes may replace the natural bait, but not often.

CHAPTER VIII

BASS FISHING WITH THE MINNOW

BASS — that is, black bass — fishing by means of the minnow, termed technically " minnow-casting," has got to be quite a distinct science, especially with the Western brethren of the rod. The rod is usually a nine-foot, or even less, lancewood or bamboo weapon, with standing guides of ample size, to allow the line easy passage through them. The line is of the best make one can afford; and the reel is a Gogebic, or Star (Fig. 43), or other fine reel constructed so that when the bait is cast its friction is of the very least, and the line runs out till the thumb stops the spool of the reel, and the minnow drops on the water. Of course, a sinker must be attached to the end of the line ; and the kind of leader, sinker, and snell I invariably use myself is shown at Fig. 70, with one to three hooks.

Now, the manner of making this cast so that the bait's head is not jerked off in the rush through the air and the termination of it, is almost, if not quite, impossible to describe. Personally, I favor the overhand cast, the motion of throwing a ball in baseball, and find it the simplest to teach the beginner. Be sure, however, to practise first with a sinker *minus* hooks and bait, on the grass or snow in winter, and you will soon get the " hang of it." If you can persuade some kind friend to give you a lesson or two, so much the better.

This method of casting the bait is distinctively American, and is never used in England, where very different styles of bait-casting prevail. These are termed the " Nottingham " and the " Thames " styles. The former is a " round arm " cast, made with both hands grasping the rod handle, and from a light wooden reel, the finger of the right hand acting as a brake on the circumference of the outer reel plate, which revolves ; the " Thames " style is more easily learnt, and for short casting may be of use to the novice.

Briefly, these are the proceedings. The rod is grasped firmly in the right hand, and a few yards of line drawn off the reel ; these are gathered in the palm of the hand in a form of the figure 8 by a reciprocating motion of the finger and thumb and ball of the hand (or lower part of the palm) and little finger, bending the wrist back and forth the while. This gathers up the line slowly for the cast; and when the point of the rod urges the bait forward, the line goes out without hindrance. It is a pretty method of fishing.

In general, bass fishing where the live minnow or other bait may be used, the "paternoster" (as it is termed in England for want of a better name) is decidedly the most useful contrivance (Fig. 70), for the simple reason that it permits of three baits of different kinds being used at one time; and the angler may attach a minnow to the bottom hook, a dobson to the next, and a frog to the highest one, with the certainty that they will be kept in motion by the moving fish. Sometimes the bass won't take a bait fish; and if this be so, even a fly can be attached to find out if they will take that. They are very capricious, especially in midsummer.

The "sink and draw" bait mentioned as useful for trout is a very good bait also for the basses, as also is the "Caledonian minnow," and "Phantom."

PICKEREL FISHING WITH A MINNOW.

Pickerel may be caught in precisely the same manner as bass ; that is, with the live minnow,

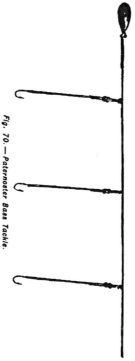

Fig. 70. — Paternoster Bass Tackle.

and with the dead " gorge " bait, or " sink and draw." Trolling with a gang is also a killing method, and requires no further instructions than are given for bass to make the method of procedure plain. The only difference consists in the necessity for using very strong tackle; and if I know I am likely to get pickerel or mascalonge, I tie my hooks to fine piano wire, otherwise, the razor-like teeth of these fish will bite through the snell. The wall-eyed pike (*Stizostedion vitreum*) is amenable to bass treatment, and in Lake Champlain and

Fig. 71.—Larvæ of Dragon Fly, or "What Is It?"

other waters is an agreeable relief, being a gamey and palatable fish.

BASS FISHING WITH DIFFERENT BAITS

Perhaps one of the most killing of baits for the bass in summer is the larva of the dragon-fly (Fig. 71). This creature is obtained from the weeds one finds in waters where the dragon-flies (or "devil's darning-needles") most frequent, and are termed by anglers, in some parts of New York,

State, " What is It ? "   The odd appearance, and the
variations in that appearance, are sufficient to puzzle the ordinary observer ; but my boy readers may

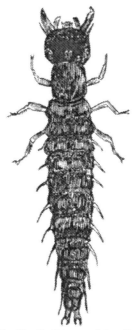

Fig. 72. — The Dobson, or Helgramite.

recognize the creature pretty surely from the above
cut.

The dobson (Fig. 72) really deserves a chapter
by itself.   It is the larva of a large fly (*Corydalus*

cornutus), and wherever it is found, there will it catch bass. Moreover, it is a very sure thing that bass will thrive in the waters that produce it, and that they are pretty generally to be found thereabouts, even as the silver birch-tree is a sign that the soil and water will do for trout. This " Dobson " has also about a score more local names ; and few boys living on the banks of bass rivers will fail to remember its decidedly interesting but pugnacious appearance.

In the winter the dobson cannot be found in the water, but hides itself deep in the earth beneath stones and *débris*, especially if the latter be woody. Early in spring it may be dug up from such positions ; but as time goes on it seeks the water and lives under stones, where it can be caught with a net of mosquito-netting. As its breathing apparatus permits it living in either air or water, it can be kept among half-rotten chips of wood in a box all summer without other food, if once a day the can or box be flooded with cool water, and this water carefully drained out again. The dobson should be hooked under the hard carapace or armor-piece at the back of the neck, taking care that you hold it firmly by the back with the left finger and thumb, or you may receive from a male dobson such a nip as will startle you, and probably cause you to drop the repulsive and savage creature in disgust. Of course this nip with the mandibles is not poisonous.

The crayfish, or, as it is sometimes termed, the fresh-water *crab*, is another very good bait for large bass. These live under the stones and woodwork incidental to mill-streams, and where they are plentiful are easy to catch in the following way : Select a dark night. Have ready some mosquito-netting tied on a wire hoop for a net. In the centre of this secure a lump of lead and a piece of fresh liver. Attach your net to a pole by means of three cords extending from it to the circumference of frame of the net, and sink it in the spot where you have reason to suspect the existence of these crayfish. Every now and then lift it suddenly, and you will find sometimes half a dozen crayfish at a time feeding on the liver. Of course if you have half a dozen nets to attend to, so much the better.

Frogs are specially good bait for bass. They are most useful when young, about an inch long, and can be kept an indefinite time in a cool place

in grass ; but you must be careful not to allow the
least chink of light, if you would save them from
vain efforts to escape. They should be hooked
under the skin of the back. A little fold only
need be pierced, and the frog will live a long time.

TROUT FISHING WITH THE GRASSHOPPER AND CRICKET.

All through the summer and autumn the angler
can find the bass and perch ready for his lures ;
and amid such a wealth of sport he must not forget that the trout fishing closes long before the
bass ceases to feed. A few golden days are there
on most streams containing the " Apollo of the
fountains," when the grasshopper and cricket are
a delicious *bonne bouche* to the trout. At such
times let my pupil collect a goodly number of
the *red*-legged grasshopper (for he it is who is
the prime favorite), and also a goodly number of the
black field-cricket. He can get the former with a
butterfly net wherever they abound, and the latter
are to be got in this wise. Strip off any pieces of
loose bark from dying trees, and lay it near to
fences where the crickets can crawl, and there be
discovered. Let the wood remain overnight, and

go early in the morning, and underneath will be
found some of the plumpest of the black crickets.
An old Vermont trout fisherman told me this, and
I have verified it. A small fine hook, very sharp,
is the best for grasshopper fishing, size No. 6 (Fig.
33).

There is one little hint in connection with this
fishing that needs imparting. When the trout
seizes the bait, he usually does so savagely, and
only to crush it. Consequently, wait until he turns
again to swallow it before you strike, and you will
catch your fish. Otherwise you will not. A dis-
abled " hopper " cast on the stream once in a
while will set the fish feeding on your hook that
is baited.

One other form of fun-making fishing occurs to
me before I close this chapter. All through the
early summer and late fall both bullheads and eels
will take a bait ; but as they are nocturnal in their
habits, it is only at night one gets really good
sport with them. Bullhead fishing is usually
practised on a dark night — preferably, just after a
heavy warm rain, and the lines are primitive
enough. Large sized eyed hooks are tied to
lines, of which two are enough for each angler.

These lines are linen braided, and have a sinker
attached to each, a loop being tied in the end.
The hook snell is also linen; and in fishing it is
best not to wait to take the hook out of the fish,
for the reason that a nasty wound may come of
handling the spiny, slimy bullhead, and a sore forefinger will certainly result from your efforts in unhooking him, if you persist in doing so.   Therefore,
I suggest tying the snell hook each time with the
tie shown (Fig. 73).   The free end at A can be

Fig. 73.— Attaching Loop and Knot for Night Fishing.

drawn out with the teeth every time, and the fish
dropped into the receptacle minus handling, which,
let me assure you, if the fish run large is no small
consideration.   Eels can be caught in precisely the
same way, and with the same tackle; and if you are
careful not to let the tail of the fish curl around
anything, he can be released at once.

Bobbing for both bullheads and eels is another
good way of fishing.   A "bob" is made by taking
a darning-needle and some worsted yarn, and

threading large worms on it, making a loose tie at intervals, and so continuing till a large, hideous squirming mass of worms is formed, more or less in the form of a ball. This is thrown overboard, attached to a stout line, and, as the fish bite, is hauled up quickly, but not too hurriedly. The fish are too voracious to let go, and, their teeth being sharp, they are drawn up, and can be lifted into the boat. Of course a lantern is necessary in all these night excursions. I cannot say I particularly care for this kind of sport, but it is sometimes amusing when no other is available.

PART IV

WINTER ANGLING

CHAPTER IX

FISHING THROUGH THE ICE

WHEN the ice king has clothed every lake and stream, and the ordinary styles of fishing can no longer be indulged in, fishing through the ice becomes at once a healthful sport, and one productive of palatable food, and possibly of a little fishing-tackle money to the juvenile angler from the sale of his superfluous capture. For this style of fishing is well fitted for the strong, healthy boy when no other occupation demands his attention. He has the glorious sunshine sparkling on the white snow; with his skates firmly attached, he can glide from tip-up to tip-up, breathing in great volumes of oxygen in the cold air; and besides this, he is catching fish, — for sure, — if he will go about it as I am about to direct.

In the first place, it is necessary to provide the tackle. The most interesting form of ice-fishing is by means of the "tip-up;" and the simplest form of this is a twig set up at an acute angle to

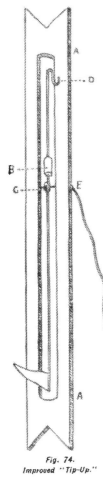

Fig. 74.
Improved "Tip-Up."

the ice, and on the tip of this is hung the line, to which a piece of red stuff has been attached. When the fish takes the bait, it pulls the piece of flag off the twig, and the angler knows at once that a fish has been at work, and runs to the hole to superintend the allowance of line the fish requires whilst pouching or swallowing the minnow. There are various reasons why the primitive form of "tip-up," however, should give place to one of more certain usefulness; and the apparatus I am about to describe out-distances the twig, as the split cane rod goes beyond the "pole" cut from the brush alongside the water.

Get some half-inch deal board and cut out pieces, as many as you require, in the shape of an outline of Fig. 74. There is no difficulty about this. Next, with a brace and bit bore two holes, one at each end, at A; then with a chisel take out the middle of each board, as shown. Now procure some stout iron wire; but previously to bending it there is a lead sinker to go on the upper end, at B. This sinker is best made by boring into the end of a piece of green hard wood, and driving a nail down into the centre of the hole for a cylindrical mould. One mould will cast a dozen or more sinkers, and the lead can be melted in a ladle over the cook-stove fire without causing inconvenience. The wire now is cut into lengths exactly the length of the space in the middle of the board, and one loop is twisted at C. Through this a nail is driven, including both sides of the board; and the wire should now swing freely round and round on this nail, as on an axle. A lead is now slipped on the upper arm of the lead (B), and a hook is formed in the wire (D). To the end of the other arm is tied a piece of old red cotton or woollen cloth, and about forty feet of stout braided linen line should be attached to the middle of the "tip-up" at E. To the other end of the line, of course, the hook is tied, which is preferably a Vir-

ginian hook not less than one-half inch across
opposite the barb, and as large as No. 1½ (Fig.
33). The tip-up is set in ice-fishing as shown
(Fig. 75). A is the line on which the hook and

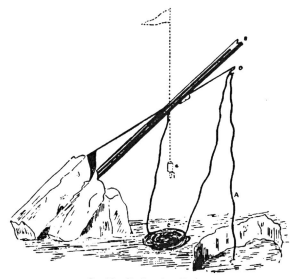

Fig. 76. — *Tip–Up set on the Ice.*

bait, plumbed so as to be sustained about one foot
from the bottom, are let down through the ice ; B
is the "tip-up," set obliquely, held by the chunks
of ice cut out of the hole ; C is the line coiled.
Observe how it works. As soon as a fish takes

the bait he pulls on the line A, which pulls down
the wire hook at D. This throws the line loose,
so that the fish can uncoil and take what it wants
of C, whilst the lead sinker slides down to the
hook on the wire (*a*), and up flies the red pen-
nant, telling to everybody interested that a fish
has bitten. (The dotted lines indicate this moment). The angler's duty now is to proceed as
fast as his legs will carry him to the tip-up, carefully ease out the line, so that the fish be not
checked, and after waiting five minutes by the
watch proceed to haul in the fish.

If these "tip-ups" are set for any length of
time, and if they be left, they will certainly be
frozen in ; and no one can do less or more than
cut them out with an axe, or wait till spring
comes. Even during the day's fishing we are
supposing, it becomes necessary to incessantly
keep the ice from accumulating or freezing in
the hole that is cut. To obviate this, and even
allow of the tip-up being set for days, I have
found the following device quite successful ; and
as it invariably happens that a fish gets on during the night or early morning, it is sometimes
quite desirable to keep the tip-ups set all the

time. Get a number of stout sticks about eigh-
teen inches long, and boring through the centre
of each at right angles, thrust about one foot of
thick iron wire through, and turn a loop in the
end (Fig. 76). When this line is set, the stick is
laid crosswise over the hole, with the rod and loop
downward (Fig. 76). Of course if the ice is
likely to be thicker than a foot, this wire ought to
be longer. It should reach into the water at least
three inches. To it is attached the line, which,
when you are setting it, is first wound up round
your thumb and finger in a figure 8 fashion, and
then attached, as shown (Fig. 77), to the pieces of
wire shaped as in Fig. 78. I think the diagrams
quite explain themselves.

The ice-fishers in Canada, and on Champlain
and the other large lakes, make a large revenue;
but it is not to that class that I am addressing
myself. On Champlain, when fishing for perch,
the eye of the fish is used almost exclusively; but
for ordinary fishing for ling, burbot, wall-eyed
pike, perch, and pickerel, small fish are the bait —
and very excellent bait they prove to be. Spear-
ing and netting through the ice are also practised;
but I find little sport or pleasure in this, and do

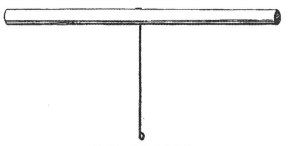

Fig. 76. — " Tip-Up " Stick.

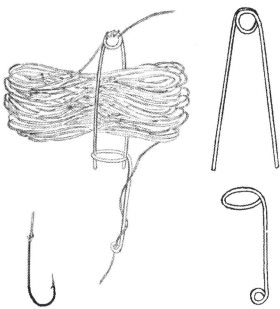

Fig. 77. — Parts of "Tip-Up."   Fig. 78. — Parts of "Tip-Up.'

not recommend my young friends to pursue it. I want them all to be true sportsmen — first, last, and all the time ; and so I have been careful that not one word in all this book gives a hint of anything but angling with a hook and line, so that the quarry the angler is pursuing for food and fun may have a good chance for its life every time.

The other forms of winter fishing possible in the South and in Great Britain are not described in this chapter. They are essentially similar to those referred to in the earlier pages ; for the seasons, of course, vary according to the latitude. What is true of the East and North, however, is, in the main, true of the West and South ; and the same methods apply pretty generally all over the country, taking into account the differences of temperature. A lengthened experience has shown me that a good fisherman in England is a good fisherman on the American continent, and a good angler in the East is a good one in the West. I shall, therefore, not enlarge further on winter fishing as it is in latitudes other than the one in which I am writing.

There is, however, yet one other kind of winter fishing that may be spoken of here. I refer to that pleasant outing we all may have in imagination, sitting before the blazing winter fire or heated stove whilst the winter gale blows snow-laden in the outer darkness. Or when busily repairing our rods, making new leaders, snelling more hooks, or neatly constructing that feather-poem, the dainty artificial fly! And how pleasant to recall the help one has been to the others because of the knowledge acquired in the ways taught by this book!

And one other instructive amusement can be followed, even in winter, beside fishing through the ice and recalling past experience — I refer to amateur fish-culture. The time will surely come when every farmer will be as fully prepared to breed fish as cattle. In the chapter on the subject included in this little book I have written with the idea of introducing trout-culture to my young readers as intensely interesting and informing, and possibly useful to them in after life. It certainly will fill up the dead season of fishing, if practised as I have laid down.

CHAPTER X

TROUT-BREEDING IN WINTER

THAT grand old angler and good Christian,
George Dawson of Albany, has put it on record
that "it is not all of fishing to fish." Similarly, I
may say, " It is not all of fish to fish." I mean,
of course, that there are many interesting points
about the fish themselves that become apparent,
aside from the actual operation of fishing. It is a
poor angler that passes his days by the waterside
intent only on filling his basket, and on simply the
capture of the fish. To him the best pleasures of
the pastime are sealed and unknown. He should
not be counted with the true disciples of the
sainted Izaak Walton ; nor is he to be considered
a true member of the "gentle craft." To such an
one fishing is fishing and nothing more. He is
like Peter Bell : " A primrose by the river's brim,
a yellow primrose was to him, and it was nothing
more." But how different with the observant fish
lover ! Every denizen of the water is to him an

object of observation and delight. He not only delights in their capture as a tribute to his own prowess, but he is an admiring possessor of the beautiful piece of watergoing architecture, than which there is no more perfect example than the trout or salmon. Taking one step farther, what could be more interesting to my young readers than the care of either of these beautiful fish from the egg up to vigorous trouthood or salmonhood? The task proposed may look a difficult one, but it really is not, as I shall demonstrate. As a boy I have done precisely as I shall describe, and subsequent experience has confirmed some conclusions which were at first tentative.

To go back to my own earliest knowledge of the subject. One of my most pleasant recollections is that of the late Mr. Frank Buckland (author of "Curiosities of Natural History," etc.) amongst his beloved infant trout at the Museum of Fish Culture, South Kensington, London, Eng. With fatherly assiduity would he attend on them; and as he brought to bear on the tiny entities the resources of his great and ingenious mind, one almost wished himself a fish, were it only to be brought within the tender care of such a fond foster-parent. Mr. Buckland's success in the breeding and rearing of fish was, as a consequence, very pronounced ; and his charming lecture before the London Royal Institution, on the subject of fish culture (which was afterwards published in book form), proves to any one that, so far from the subject being a dull one, it is replete with remarkable interest, and far from difficult of practice.

Of course, however, it is impossible for boys in general to undertake the artificial spawning, impregnation, rearing, feeding, etc., on the scale carried out in the various State hatcheries ; but, as I shall explain in the following pages, it is quite within the means of my readers to artificially hatch and rear a few dozen of trout or young salmon ; and what can be a prettier or more interesting amusement for the student of fish-life, apart from the knowledge it imparts of the natural history of the most important family of fishes in the world ? Boys breed and rear canaries and other birds, rabbits, guinea-pigs, mice, and dogs ; why, therefore, should fish be neglected, when they are really easier to breed and keep than any of those just named ? And are they not far more beautiful ?

What can form a more lovely pet than a tame carmine-spotted trout taking its food from your fingers? I intend, therefore, giving plain directions, by means of which any one possessed of ingenuity and a little careful patience may satisfactorily become a trout and salmon breeder on a small scale at a very little cost ; and, as the chief part of the operations will be carried out during the winter, when outdoor sports are few, I feel sure my instructions will not fall to the ground.

First, I must recapitulate briefly the natural history of the salmon family. Now, all this family, which consists of several species of trout and the lordly salmon himself as the head, have habits as regards food, places of habitation, spawning, feeding, etc., very similar to each other. As winter approaches, unlike many other fish of our rivers, which spawn in summer, the trout or salmon ascends the river and proceeds to make a nest in the gravel. " Fancy," I think I hear some one say, "a fish making a nest. I thought it was only birds did that." Quite incorrect, my young friend ; the trout and salmon make a distinct nest in the gravel, not of fibres it is true (the stickle-back does that, however), but by turning up the stones by means of a sort of undulating movement from head to tail. Both male and female assist in this ; and when a suitable cavity is formed, the female deposits the eggs, which are about the size of a small pea, and of a beautiful salmon-flesh color. The male then impregnates them, and they both set to and cover them up. After about a hundred days the eggs burst, letting out the tiny fish, which for a considerable time lie helpless, feeding only by absorption from an oil-bag, or vesicle, which in time becomes the stomach of the perfectly formed fish. After this it feeds, and takes its chance in the struggle for existence.

Such is a short history of the natural process of breeding. The artificial method, of which the lamented Seth Green and his yet living brother and others were and are apostles, consists in taking a fish full of spawn and catching the eggs from it in a suitable vessel. These are then impregnated and passed on in an artificial stream of water until they hatch, after which, as soon as they can feed, they are fed, and so grown on. It is a part of the artificial method I am going to explain.

The artificial spawning of fish is manifestly impracticable for most of my readers ; but as there are many gentlemen who sell ova, or eggs, they may be procured without difficulty,[1] and I will therefore commence from the period when the eggs are actually in progress towards hatching.

The apparatus first commands our closest attention. A constant stream of water is indispensable at the outset, and the next requisite is a suitable box or boxes for the reception of the ova and the fry when they appear. Neither of these is difficult to obtain.

As to the water. If it be possible to join on a pipe to the water-works' supply, and regulate the stream of water by means of a tap, then half the battle is won; but as it is not likely that boys will care to purposely go to this expense, some other device must be thought of. A cistern, or even tub, if clean and sweet, will do to store the water in, if the latter is pumped from a well; and it should be indoors, out of the reach of frost, and raised above your boxes or troughs. It need not necessarily be very near, for a small India-rubber pipe will convey all the water.

I have said that it should be indoors; that is, in

[1] J. Annin, Jr., Caledonia, Livingstone Co., N.Y., supplies eggs and fry in the proper season.

an out-house or cellar, of course, because if it were
out the frost might stop the supply of water during the night, and kill all your fish in a few hours.
I will suppose you have a tool-shed, or part of
a barn, therefore, at your disposal. Of course a
good and reliable stove must be fixed ; that is a
prime essential. This is how I would go to work
in the very cheapest way. Fix in one corner, at
about five feet from the floor, two stout iron
brackets. Procure a cask ; a molasses cask will
do. Have the head knocked in, and the inside
thoroughly cleansed with boiling water, and after
that deeply charred ; the charcoal thus formed
clears the water of impurity. The charring is
done with hot embers from the stove. Set the
barrel upon your brackets securely, and be sure
they are strong enough to bear the weight of the
water. You have thus your water receptacle,
which will, of course, require refilling as it empties
(Fig. 79). Now, before going farther, just let me
make two or three remarks on this important subject of water supply. Of course, when advising
the purchase and fixing of a barrel, I am supposing that no house-tank is accessible, and that my
reader depends upon an artificial supply. Of

course, also, a zinc or lead, or even wood, tank
would do better, though not much. Besides, the
barrel is always useful long after my experimen-
talist has given up fish-breeding. Just, however,
as it is certain a kennel is necessary for a dog, or
a hutch for rabbits, so is the barrel or reservoir

Fig. 79. — Water Cask.

necessary for the fish, and, as I have recommended, does not come very high.

We will now suppose the cask is fixed; the next
thing is a covering or lid to keep out the dust.
Anything that suggests itself as suitable will do

for this, so nothing further need be said about it. The arrangement for an outlet must now be made. An ordinary wooden faucet will do capitally; but you must boil it in water for some time before using it, in order to extract any sap, etc., in the wood likely to taint the water. When dry, drive it into a hole previously bored at a distance

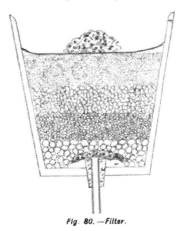

Fig. 80. — Filter.

of about six inches from the bottom. An India rubber pipe will connect this with your next necessary article, namely, a filter; for trout must have the purest water when they are very young.

Now, the filter (Fig. 80) is very easily made in this wise. Procure a large flower-pot, the largest

you can get. Make a wire tripod stand for it of
about a foot in height. Into the hole at the
bottom of the pot insert a cork, through which a
glass pipe (easily procurable at your drug-store) of
about three inches long has been inserted. You
can bore the cork through with a red-hot iron,
and be careful that it is a good sound one ; also
be very sure that it fits the aperture exactly, so
that no water can escape except through the pipe.
The latter should be at least three-eighths of
an inch in diameter, inside measurement, or the
supply of water will be inadequate to the demands of health in the fish. When the cork is
inserted, the glass pipe should be flush or even
with that part of it inside the flower-pot, and the
rest outside. On the outside length your India-
rubber piping will be attached.

The making of the filter, from which we have
slightly digressed, is as follows : Having arranged
the cork and glass as I have directed, immediately
above the latter, inside the pot, a piece of well-
washed, fine sponge, not larger than a slice from
an orange of say half-inch thickness, should be
placed. Immediately on this a half-inch layer of
well-washed stones of not more than three-eighths

of an inch in diameter are placed ; they may grad-
uate, of course, to lesser sizes. Thereafter follows
a layer of at least an inch and 'a half of smaller
stones, the limit of size being a pea, and the minimum being a mustard seed. Next a layer of
wood charcoal, broken up into small pieces ; next
a layer of sand, well washed before using, and
finally a piece of coarse muslin. Another piece
of sponge may be placed at the top to break the
fall of the water from the cistern. Here, therefore, is a splendidly efficient filter, which will,
however, I must say, require cleaning out occasionally, more or less frequently, in fact, according
to the purity or impurity of the water. In view
of this, perhaps it is well to make two or three
others at the same time, so that the fish may
never have impure water.

The stream of water is now assured, and its
purity certain. The next concern, of course, is
the troughs or tanks in which the eggs are to be
kept and matured into life. These are constructed
of various materials, and so used by the professed
fish culturist, slate, glass, earthenware, and wood
being chiefly in requisition. For the present
purpose wood is quite good enough. Let me

first, however, describe what the trough is when adapted for its use. It consists of a receptacle, say, six inches deep, of a rectangular shape, in which the ova are stored, fitted to receive water, and also furnished with a spout from which the overflow emerges. This is how it is made, and I do not think I can be too terse and practical. Take (for our present purpose) three lengths of well-seasoned pine plank half an inch thick by three feet long by ten inches for one, and the others nine inches broad. The ten-inch wood plank will form the bottom, and the other two the sides. Two other ten-inch-by-nine pieces of the same kind of wood are necessary to form the ends. These parts should be put together with copper nails such as boat-builders use, and no corrosion in consequence ensues, as would be the case were iron nails employed. Iron nails will do, however, if the copper are not available.

After the box has been made so securely that no water can escape, the next operation is that of charring the interior. It is a well-known fact amongst pisciculturists that the charred wood box or trough presents more lively fish than any other kind of apparatus. Well, the charring process is easy enough. Take out the red-hot embers of a good coal fire and place them in a box, moving them as it is found the wood ignites. Some care and perseverance are necessary to char the interior properly; but it can, of course, be done without more difficulty than a certain amount of patience and dexterity in themselves indicate. The idea is to make the inside of the trough a perfect lining of charcoal, so that no fungus or other impurity can exist. Curious, isn't it, that carbon, or charcoal, is one of the most powerful antiseptics of nature, and that vegetable growths and all impurities will not attach themselves to it? or, if the latter do, they lose all their vicious character and become innocuous. Mr. Monroe Green of the Caledonia Hatchery, N.Y., uses a coating of coal-tar only, and finds it all that is required.

Thus your trough is finished, excepting the all-necessary outlet. In order to make this, bore a hole seven-eighths of an inch in diameter, and with a cement of white lead introduce a short length of lead pipe. Now, the white lead must be used sparingly, and as little as possible should be allowed to appear on the water side of the trough. It must also be allowed to become hard before the receptacle is put in use ; and if sufficient care be exercised in this, there is but little fear of the lead proving deleterious to the fish. A slanting section of the pipe may be cut off by means of a good sharp knife or saw ; and trough, spout, and all is then furnished with sufficient complete ness to rear the most delicate of all fishes (Fig. 81).

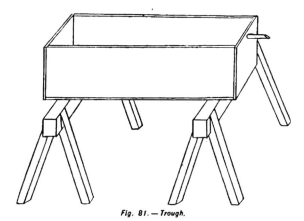

Fig. 81. — Trough.

In large fish-breeding establishments a series of troughs, either of slate, glass, earthenware, or, as I have just described, of wood, is usually erected and the water passes, by means of the spouts, from end to end of each. This series may, and often does, number ten or a dozen troughs, and, of course, admits of a great number of fry being hatched. I am, however, writing for boys here, and I do not advise a larger receptacle than that described, for an initial experiment. Such a trough will accommodate some thousands of ova at a pinch, though I advise the learner not to, in any case, overcrowd. The fewer the eggs under care, the easier is each individual looked after, and the easier is it to remove dead matter, *débris*, and the ordinary flotsam and jetsam inevitable on an assemblage of living beings.

The trough I have described should be placed on either trestle, or on stakes driven into the ground, to a height which, whilst it admits of a fairly good fall from the cistern to the filter, is not too low so as to be inconvenient. In my fish-breeding experiment nothing has seemed to conduce to the lack of patient, absorbed observation of the eggs and embryos like the backache engendered by reason of the inconveniently low troughs ; therefore, be particular when making your trestles not to make the legs too short. The trough can be nailed (copper nails preferable) to the stakes or trestle for security's sake ; in fact, it is advisable this should be done. I once had a terrible disaster when I first began, as a boy, to artificially hatch fish. My coat happened to catch in a corner of the trough, and the whole bag of tricks came splash over me, costing me the death of at least a hundred young fish. As these were worth about two cents each, I can leave my reader to imagine the lesson it taught.

The tank which is to receive the young fish when their period of absorption-feeding is past, and when they begin to eat with their mouths, when, in fact, they are to be fed and brought up till of sufficient age to be transported to the aquarium, pond, or stream, must be of larger dimensions than the hatching-trough. I recommend, therefore, that it be made of deal, as before, which can be charred or not, and of these dimensions : one foot deep, four feet broad by six feet long. Six clear inches of water is quite sufficient for these young gentlemen ; and an outlet, as recommended for the hatching-trough, which communicates with a drain, is necessary. Before and over both the openings in the trough, and that in this "stew," or tank, it is important to bear in mind that a zinc-wire covering must be fixed at some distance from both. The object of both these contrivances is to keep the tiny embryos and fry from passing away from their allotted dwelling-places, which, with a perverseness of all young organisms, they would inevitably do were they left to their own devices.

Coverings of wood must also be provided for both these receptacles ; for it is found that eggs hatch better in darkness, and the young alevins are intolerant of light. With the fry the precaution is not so necessary, except for the purpose of keeping away all nocturnal enemies. An old cat once played me a pretty trick, catching and eating a lot of my two-inch fry ; and a rat once did worse than that, — he simply gnawed a hole in the bottom of the tank, and when it was empty hopped in and devoured the lot of fish, remaining high and dry.

I have now described the chief apparatus, which, to recapitulate, consists of a reservoir, a filter, a hatching-trough, and a "stew," or tank, for the fish when they have arrived at the feeding-age. Place them in order, and turn on your water for a day or two to sweeten the whole affair. This done, it becomes necessary to see about stocking the hatching-trough. First, however, procure some nice sharp gravel ; the stones should not be larger than peas, and as uniform in size as possible. They should be boiled (not to render them soft, of course), to clear off and kill any impurity. Having thereafter washed them carefully in several waters, spread a layer of about an inch in thickness over the bottom of your two receptacles. It is not really necessary to do this in the "stew" until you are ready to receive the fry in it. However, as it is scarcely necessary to take two bites off one cherry, it may be better, perhaps, to do both at the same time. Having done this, obtain some larger stones, ranging from the size of a filbert to that of a plum, and place these sparely, so that, as the water passes over them, tiny eddies may be formed. These are of very salutary value to young trout or salmon, and serve the purpose of shelter and quietude.

I have said that the art of spawning and impregnating is impracticable for most boys. This being so, and as there are gentlemen who make a business of supplying eyed ova, I can only repeat my advice as to the purchase of the eggs from a reliable fish culturist. As a rule, the eggs are retained by the vendor until the two eyes of the little fish, which are large and unmistakable, can be seen through the shell of the egg. If the ova are removed before this the chances of their dying are very great ; and when " eyed," however, the chances are just oppositely small, insomuch as that as many as ninety-five per cent may be safely received off a journey of one hundred miles if they have been packed with judgment and care.

Let us suppose the tyro has purchased, say, one thousand eyed eggs, and has his apparatus in order, with a gentle stream dribbling into his hatching-trough. The eggs will, doubtless, come to him in damp moss, and no time should be lost in introducing them to their future home. This is done in no extraordinary manner ; the ova being only turned in and distributed over the gravel by means of a feather. Be careful in doing this to spread the tiny opaline beads so that they do not bunch, but are well apart. Having done this, replace the cover of your trough, and let them have twelve hours clear rest before you again look at them.

On again closely scanning them you may perchance notice one or two of a different color to the rest ; that is, they are whitish, as if addled. These are dead, and must be removed. To do